Animal

Christmas
Collection

Pets' Party
Kitten Kisses
Spaniel Surprise

Illustrations by Paul Howard

LUCY DANIELS

Hodder
Children's
Books

A division of Hachette Children's Books

This edition of Pets' Party first published as a single volume in 1998
This edition of Kitten Kisses first published as a single volume in 2002
This edition of Spaniel Surprises first published as a single volume in 2000

This edition published in 2013

Pets' Party

Special thanks to Helen Magee

Animal Ark is a registered trademark of Working Partners Ltd.
Text copyright © 1998 Ben M. Baglio
Original series created by Ben M. Baglio, London Q12 7QY
Illustrations copyright © 1998 Paul Howard

The right of Lucy Daniels to be identified as the author of
this work has been asserted by her in accordance with the
Copyright, Designs and Patents Act 1988.

For more information about Animal Ark please contact www.animalark.co.uk
1

All rights reserved. Apart from any use permitted under UK copyright law,
this publication may only be reproduced, stored or transmitted, in any form,
or by any means with prior permission in writing of the publishers or in the
case of reprographic production in accordance with the terms of licences
issued by the Copyright Licensing Agency and may not be otherwise
circulated in any form of binding or cover other than that in which it is
published and without a similar condition being imposed on the
subsequent purchaser.

All characters in this publication are fictitious and any resemblance
to real persons, living or dead, is purely coincidental.

A Catalogue record for this book is available from the British Library

ISBN 978 1 444 91608 9

Typeset in Bembo by Avon DataSet Ltd, Bidford-on-Avon, Warwickshire

Printed and bound in Great Britain by
Clays Ltd, St Ives plc

The paper and board used in this paperback by Hodder
Children's Books are natural recyclable products made from
wood grown in sustainable forests. The manufacturing processes
conform to the environmental regulations of the country of origin.

Hodder Children's Books
a division of Hachette Children's Books
338 Euston Road, London NW1 3BH
An Hachette UK company

www.hodderchildrens.co.uk

Pets' Party

1

A new boy at school

"Come on, James, the bell's gone." Mandy Hope shivered as she called over her shoulder to her best friend. She could feel her cheeks glowing red. The wind was blowing cold off the moors that surrounded the village of Welford. Mandy was glad of the bright woolly scarf Gran had knitted for her. It kept her cosy even in the chilliest of winds.

It's nearly Christmas, Mandy thought happily. Maybe there would be snow soon. James Hunter ran through the school gate behind her. As he went, he skidded on a patch of ice and bumped into a thin, elderly lady. She was muffled up in a long black coat and had a black felt hat pulled down over her ears.

"Sorry, Mrs Trigg," James apologised.

Mrs Trigg gave James a severe look. "Really, James, why weren't you looking where you were going?" she asked sternly.

"I slipped on some ice," James protested.

"You shouldn't have been running," Mrs Trigg replied. "You children are always running everywhere. Max is just the same."

Max, Mandy thought. *Mrs Trigg's grandson.* Mrs Trigg lived in Holly Cottage, near to Lilac Cottage where Mandy's gran and grandad lived. Mandy's gran had told her that Max was coming to stay with his gran until after Christmas, because his dad was working away and his mum had gone into hospital.

"Hello, Mrs Trigg," Mandy said. "Has

your grandson arrived yet?"

"I've just left him with his teacher," Mrs Trigg replied. "He's going to be in Mrs Todd's class."

Mandy nodded. "Mrs Todd is my teacher too," she said. "I'll look after Max if you like. James and I can introduce him to *everybody*!"

Mrs Trigg smiled. "That would be very kind, Mandy," she said. "I thought it would do him good to spend the week before the Christmas holidays at school with all the other children. *I* won't be much company for him."

Mandy smiled back, pleased. Mrs Trigg hardly ever smiled; she usually looked worried. Mandy thought she seemed much nicer when she smiled.

"It'll be lovely for you having Max to stay, won't it?" Mandy said. "I'm sure he'll enjoy it too."

"I hope so," Mrs Trigg replied. Then she sighed. "It's that dog of his that really worries me. It's going to be such trouble."

"Dog!" Mandy exclaimed. "He's brought a dog with him?" Mandy loved animals, which was just as well, as her parents were vets in Welford. They lived in Animal Ark, a stone-built cottage with a surgery attached. Mandy loved meeting all her parents' animal patients.

"I've told Max the dog has to sleep in the potting shed," Mrs Trigg went on. "I don't want all the mess and bother that pets make."

Mandy bit back her reply. Because Animal Ark was so busy with animal patients,

Mandy wasn't allowed a pet for the time being, though she would have loved one. She couldn't imagine a pet ever being a bother.

"Come on, Mandy," James urged her. "The bell went ages ago."

Mandy waved goodbye to Mrs Trigg and raced into school. She couldn't wait to meet Max's dog. A cold gust of wind blew as she crossed the school yard. She shivered and pulled her soft, red scarf up to her chin. Imagine making a dog sleep in the potting shed in this weather. Poor thing!

"What's your dog's name?" Mandy asked Max at morning playtime.

Everyone had crowded round Max, telling him all about Welford and trying to make him welcome.

"Sandy," Max replied. "He's a Cairn terrier. My dad gave him to me before he went to work abroad. He's six months old now."

"So he's still a puppy!" Mandy exclaimed delightedly.

"Peter's got a Cairn, too. He's called Timmy," James told Max.

"But Timmy's more of a *terror* than a *terrier*," Peter Foster added, grinning. "He's the naughtiest dog in Welford."

Max's big blue eyes lit up. "Cairns aren't really naughty," he said. "They've just got lots of energy. Maybe Sandy and Timmy could be friends."

"And James has a Labrador. His name is Blackie," Mandy told Max. "Blackie *loves* making friends with other dogs."

"I bet Blackie doesn't have to sleep in the potting shed," Max said.

"Of course he doesn't," James replied fiercely. Then he looked sympathetically at Max. "Your gran told us that Sandy had to. Won't she let him into the house at all?"

Max shook his head. His eyes looked sad. "She thinks he would make too much mess."

Mandy felt very sorry for Max. "Why don't you bring Sandy round to Animal Ark?" she suggested. "And we can take him and Blackie out for walks. Blackie would love that, wouldn't he, James?"

James nodded. "And you can bring him carol singing the day before Christmas Eve," he added. "There will be loads of us going round the village, and everyone is going to bring their pets."

"I won't be able to bring Toto though," Jill Redfern said. "Toto is a tortoise and tortoises hibernate in winter."

"But I'm bringing Duchess, my Persian cat," said Richard Tanner.

"And I'm bringing Minnie, my mouse," Amy Fenton piped up. "Of course, I'll have to wrap her up warmly."

Mandy smiled and looked up at the sky. "Do you think there will be snow for Christmas?" she asked.

"I hope so," Max said. "At least then it will seem a bit more *like* Christmas." Then his face fell. "But then it might be too cold for Sandy in the potting shed."

Mandy looked at him in concern. "You aren't unhappy at Holly Cottage, are you?" she asked.

Max looked at the floor, then back at

Mandy. "Not really," he said. "I love my gran but it isn't like being at home. Mum and Dad don't mind if Sandy jumps on the furniture or anything, but Gran is so fussy about things like that. And she doesn't even have a Christmas tree. Mum and Dad and I decorate a Christmas tree every year and now I won't be with them for Christmas. Dad is working abroad and he isn't sure if he'll be able to get home for Christmas. And now Mum might not be home either." Max looked even more sad.

"I'll tell you what," Mandy suggested.

"James and I are going round to *my* gran's after school for tea. She lives at Lilac Cottage, just down from your gran's. Why don't we bring Blackie to meet Sandy afterwards?"

"Would you?" asked Max. "I'd really like that – and so would Sandy."

"It's a date," said Mandy. "And I promise you, Max, you're going to have a great Christmas in Welford. We'll make sure of it, won't we, everybody?" Mandy looked round at her friends. They all nodded in agreement.

"Of course we will," Gary Roberts said. "You can come and see Gertie, my garter-snake if you like."

"How would you like to have a ride on Paddy, my pony?" Paul Stevens asked.

Max laughed. "I'd love it," he replied. "Is Welford full of animals?"

"Just wait till you see Animal Ark," Mandy told him. "At the moment we've got a parrot and a rabbit, two kittens and a gerbil, a hamster, a budgie and three guinea-pigs."

"Wow!" said Max. "You're going to have a full house for Christmas."

Mandy shook her head. "Mum and Dad like to send as many animals as possible home at Christmas," she explained. "They're working really hard to get them all well enough to go back to their owners by Christmas Eve."

"I'll have to hurry if I want to see all the animals before they leave then," said Max. "Can I really come to Animal Ark?"

"So long as you promise to bring Sandy," Mandy insisted.

"That's no problem," Max replied, smiling. "Sandy and I go everywhere together."

The bell rang for the end of playtime and Mandy looked across at James. He gave her the thumbs-up sign. If it was up to Welford Village Primary School, Max was going to have a very good Christmas indeed! But one thing still troubled Mandy. Sandy's Christmas would be no fun at all if Mrs Trigg had anything to do with it. Mandy couldn't bear the thought of the poor puppy out in the cold potting shed on his own. She frowned. Somehow she had to change Mrs Trigg's mind!

2

Meeting Sandy

"Just imagine it, Gran!" Mandy wailed when she and James were at Lilac Cottage having tea. "Sandy has to sleep in the potting shed!"

"Now, now, Mandy," Grandad put in. "I'm sure Maggie Trigg has got a snug, warm bed made up for the little fellow. She's a kind woman. She would never be cruel to an animal."

"She's just very house-proud," Gran said, putting a plate of cheese sandwiches, and another one of home-made ginger cake, on the table.

James slipped a bit of cheese sandwich to Blackie. The Labrador pup gobbled it up and thumped his tail on the floor. At least *Blackie* was happy!

Mandy sighed. "Why doesn't Mrs Trigg like animals, Gran?"

Gran shrugged. "I don't think Maggie dislikes animals," she replied. "I would imagine that she just thinks they make a lot of mess. You know, she used to be a rather jolly, happy-go-lucky sort of person. She used to enjoy coming to the Women's Institute with me."

"And she used to be very involved in Welford's amateur dramatic society," Grandad added.

"Mrs Trigg?" exclaimed Mandy.

Grandad nodded. "Maggie and her husband, Bill, directed the Christmas panto every year in the church hall," he went on. "But a few years ago Bill died, and since then Maggie seems to have lost interest in everything, poor woman."

"She doesn't get involved with anything any more," Gran agreed. "She spends all her time cleaning her house. It's as if she decided to put all her love and care into Holly Cottage."

"I think it will be good for Maggie to have Max staying with her," Grandad said thoughtfully. "It'll give her someone else to care for."

"You could be right, Tom," Mandy's gran replied. "I think she's lonely."

"So why doesn't she get a pet?" Mandy asked, helping herself to a large piece of ginger cake. "No, don't tell me – it would make too much mess." She sighed again. "Do you think Mrs Trigg will ever change her mind about animals?"

Grandad ruffled Mandy's short fair hair. "Are you going to make a project out of Maggie Trigg?" he asked, his eyes twinkling.

Mandy stopped chewing for a moment. "Maybe I will," she said. "Maybe that's *just* what I'll do."

James shoved his glasses up on his nose and rolled his eyes. "Uh-oh," he said. "Poor Mrs Trigg."

"Poor Sandy!" Mandy retorted. Then she smiled. "Let's go! I can't wait to meet him!"

Mandy and James raced a few houses down the lane to Holly Cottage. Blackie bounded along beside them, enjoying the run.

"There's somebody in the potting shed," James said, as they went through the gate.

Warm yellow light spilled out of the window of the potting shed on to the path. The winter afternoon was growing dark and the little shed looked cosy.

Max popped his head round the potting shed door as he heard their voices. "In here," he said. "Sandy is waiting for you."

Mandy ran towards the shed door and a furry bundle launched itself at her. "Oh, aren't you gorgeous!" she exclaimed as Sandy jumped up and put his two front paws on her legs. "I can see why you call him Sandy, Max."

The little terrier was a pale golden colour.

His shaggy coat looked thick and well groomed. Max obviously took very good care of his pet. Mandy bent down and fussed over Sandy, rubbing his ears. The puppy rolled over on to his back and she tickled his tummy.

Blackie scampered into the shed after James. The Labrador wagged his tail furiously when he saw Sandy.

"Hey, watch out!" Max said, grabbing a packet of seeds that Blackie's tail had knocked off a low shelf.

Blackie took no notice. He was already

snuffling at Sandy's nose, butting the other pup playfully. Sandy sprang up and butted Blackie back. Soon the two dogs were rolling on the potting shed floor, playing and getting to know each other.

James laughed. "I reckon they're friends already," he remarked.

Max looked proudly at his pet. "Sandy just loves company," he said. "I hate leaving him in here on his own."

Mandy looked round the shed. There was a dog basket in one corner with a warm, woolly blanket inside. Beside it was a food bowl, a water bowl and a hot-water bottle.

"I put the hot-water bottle there in case he gets cold during the night," Max told them.

Mandy looked at Max sympathetically. "You've made the shed really comfortable for him," she said. "I'm sure he'll be all right. Cairn terriers have lovely thick, warm coats."

Max's mouth drooped. "It's just that I'm so used to having him around," he explained. "What if he misses me during the night? He'll howl his head off. And what about during the day when I'm at school? Who's going to take him for a walk? He'll probably cry all day."

James frowned. "Your gran won't like that," he said.

"Max!" called a voice from the back door of the cottage. "Max, where are you?"

"In the potting shed, Gran," Max called back. "Mandy and James have come to visit Sandy."

Mrs Trigg peered out from the kitchen door. "It's cold out there," she said. "Come inside." The old lady turned and went back into the house.

Blackie sat up, his ears pricked. Before James could stop him, the Labrador had galloped up the path and into the cottage.

"Uh-oh," said James. "Blackie, come back!"

Sandy gave a short bark and raced up the path after Blackie.

"Sandy!" Max shouted. But both dogs had disappeared.

Mandy, James and Max all dived out

through the door of the shed, hurtling up the path after the dogs. Mandy got to the kitchen door first, and winced as she heard a dreadful clatter.

Mrs Trigg was standing in the middle of the kitchen, looking very annoyed. A pot stand had been overturned and the floor was littered with pots and pans. "*Now* do you see why I don't let dogs in the house, Max?" Mrs Trigg said, as he came into the kitchen with James. "Look what those dogs have done. I'm beginning to think it would be better to send Sandy to kennels if he's going to behave like this."

Max gasped. "Oh, no, Gran!" he pleaded, as he bent down to pick up the pots and pans. "Sandy didn't mean any harm. I'll clear this up. Please don't send him away."

Mrs Trigg looked at Max's white, worried face, and her own stern expression softened just a little. "Now, now," she said. "There's no need to get so upset over an animal, Max."

"But he isn't just an animal," Max protested. "He's *Sandy*. Dad gave him to me before he went to work abroad, and I promised Mum I would take good care of him while she was in hospital. I'm all he's got just now!" Mandy could see that he was holding back his tears.

Mrs Trigg looked shocked at Max's outburst. "Oh dear," she sighed, ruffling her grandson's hair. "You're missing your mum and dad a lot, aren't you?" She didn't seem angry any more.

Max nodded. "Do you think maybe Mum will be out of hospital for Christmas?" he asked.

"I'm afraid not, Max," she said softly. "I rang the hospital today and they don't think that's very likely."

Max hung his head and Sandy reached up to him, licking his hand. "Oh, Sandy," Max said, burying his face in Sandy's neck.

Mrs Trigg's expression softened as she looked at Max and Sandy. "Don't worry about the kennels, Max," she said. "We'll manage somehow."

"You mean you won't send him away?" Max asked hopefully.

Mrs Trigg sighed and set the pot stand upright. "Not if he behaves himself," she said at last, looking down at the puppy. Sandy put his head on one side and looked appealingly up at Mrs Trigg. "Bad dog!" she said to him. But Mandy noticed the old lady couldn't help smiling a little as she helped Max replace the pots and pans.

Sandy scampered over to Mrs Trigg and began trying to undo her shoe laces, wagging his stumpy tail. He put a paw on top of her left foot and rubbed his head against her ankle. Mandy was pleased to see that Mrs

Trigg didn't push the puppy away.

Max scooped him up. "I'll take him back to the potting shed," he said. "He'll be good, I promise, Gran."

Mrs Trigg shook her head. "Come near the fire and get warm first. You can take him out later. Leave him in here in the kitchen for now. Come on, all of you."

James looked at Mandy as Mrs Trigg led the way out of the kitchen. "Where's Blackie?" he mouthed.

Mandy gasped. "I'd forgotten about Blackie," she confessed. "Where on earth has he got to?"

3

Pets in trouble!

Mrs Trigg's voice floated back to them from the living-room. "Well, of all the cheek!" she exclaimed.

Mandy and James hurried into the living-room behind her. "Oh, no!" said James.

Blackie was stretched out on the sofa in front of the fire. His eyes were closed and he was snoozing peacefully. An embarrassed

James collared Blackie and dragged him off.

"Just look at all the dog hairs over my sofa," Mrs Trigg complained.

"Sorry, Mrs Trigg," James apologised.

While Mrs Trigg went to get a brush, Mandy cast a quick look round the living-room. The fire burned brightly in the grate, but everything was too neat and tidy to be comfortable and welcoming. There wasn't a Christmas decoration in sight and, worst of all, no Christmas tree.

"I guess we'd better be going," Mandy said to Max.

Max nodded. "I'll see you tomorrow at school," he replied.

"Why don't you come to Animal Ark for tea?" Mandy suggested, as Mrs Trigg came back into the room with a dustpan and brush. "Grandad will walk over to Animal Ark with you; he's coming round anyway. And bring Sandy. Then we can go to carol practice together afterwards."

The carol singers had arranged a practice session at the village hall. Mrs Ponsonby had promised to supervise them, and coach them! Mrs Ponsonby was chairwoman of the Welford Women's Institute. She always liked to get involved in anything that was happening in the village. In fact, she usually reckoned she should be in charge.

"Can I go with Sandy to Mandy's house for tea tomorrow, Gran?" Max asked. "Mandy's grandad will walk me round there."

"Haven't your mum and dad got enough animals to look after, without Sandy getting under their feet?" Mrs Trigg asked Mandy.

Mandy smiled. "Oh, no," she assured Mrs Trigg. "They won't mind at all. They love animals – and they'll adore Sandy. He's so sweet."

Mrs Trigg looked unsure. "I don't know about sweet," she said. "Animals just make a mess as far as I can see."

"But they're such good companions," Mandy went on. "Mrs Ponsonby is always saying how lonely she would be without Pandora." Mrs Ponsonby might be the bossiest woman in Welford, but she really loved Pandora, her Pekinese.

Mrs Trigg looked thoughtful as she bent to brush the dog hairs off the sofa. James nudged Mandy and she followed his eyes. Sandy had crept into the room after Mrs Trigg. He stretched a paw up to the low coffee table where Mrs Trigg's knitting lay neatly rolled up. Before Max could get to him he had loosened the ball of wool and it had dropped to the floor. Sandy scampered after it just as Mrs Trigg turned round.

"No!" she said sternly to the little dog as he made to pounce on the ball of wool. "Sit!"

Sandy looked up at her, then sat down obediently, his head on one side. As Mrs Trigg bent down to pick up her wool, the little dog lifted his right paw and held it out to her.

Mandy couldn't help smiling; he looked so adorable.

"That's a trick I taught him," Max said proudly. "He wants to shake hands, Gran."

"Hmmph," said Mrs Trigg. Rather stiffly, she quickly "shook hands" with Sandy, then wiped her hand on her apron. "You'd be

better teaching him to do as he's told," she added.

"But he *did*, Mrs Trigg," Mandy put in. "He sat down when you told him, and he hasn't even touched the ball of wool."

Mrs Trigg stood with the dustpan and brush in her hand, looking at Sandy. "I suppose you're right, Mandy," she admitted. "He obviously recognises a firm tone of voice."

James looked out of the window. "Oh, look!" he said. "It's started to snow. We can go sledging at the weekend if it settles."

Mandy and Max rushed to the window. Big fat flakes of snow were falling, swirling in the light from the window.

"Isn't it lovely?" Mandy breathed. "It's so *Christmassy*!"

"But it makes a terrible mess when it melts," Mrs Trigg said.

Mandy looked at the old woman. Her dark navy cardigan was buttoned right up to the neck and the white collar of her blouse was crisp and neat. Her skirt was dark and neat too. Even her apron looked as if it had been starched and pressed. Everything about her was neat and buttoned-up. Her short grey hair was tucked behind her ears – neatly!

"But the snow is beautiful while it lasts, Mrs Trigg," Mandy said. "Don't you think so?"

Mrs Trigg came to stand beside them. She turned her face up to watch the snowflakes falling. "Your grandad used to love snow, Max," she said softly. "You probably don't remember, but when you were a very little boy he made a snowman with you out in the garden there."

Mandy looked at Mrs Trigg. Her face was softer somehow – as if she was remembering a lot of happy things.

Sandy had scampered up to join them. Max picked him up and looked up at his gran. "I remember," he said. "Grandad made me the best snowman in the world." Mrs Trigg put her arm around her grandson's shoulder and hugged him.

"We'd better go," Mandy said quietly.

"Shall I take Sandy out to the potting

shed then?" Max asked his gran reluctantly.

Sandy lifted his head and licked Mrs Trigg's hand. The old woman drew her hand away, wiping it on her apron again. But then she said briskly, "Maybe we'd better let him sleep in the warm kitchen tonight."

"Oh thanks, Gran!" Max said, his face lighting up.

Mrs Trigg smiled at her grandson. "But I won't have him in the rest of the house," she warned. "I can't do with all these dog hairs around," she said, giving Blackie a stern look.

Mandy and James grinned at each other. Max was cuddling Sandy as if he would never let him go, and Mrs Trigg was bustling about, sweeping up more invisible dog hairs.

"Come on, Blackie," James said. "Let's go home. See you tomorrow, Max."

The carol singers gathered in the village hall the following afternoon. James and Max had brought Blackie and Sandy, and Peter Foster had turned up with Timmy, his Cairn terrier. The others had left their pets at home until the big day. Mrs Ponsonby couldn't complain about the dogs being there: she had brought Pandora.

"*Hark! the herald-angels sing . . .*" sang the carol singers.

Mrs Ponsonby stood in front of them, waving her arms around. "Louder!" she boomed. "*Glory to the new-born King!*" Her voice wavered on the high notes and Mandy suppressed a giggle. Blackie began to howl as Mrs Ponsonby's voice wobbled through the carol.

"At least Mrs Ponsonby isn't coming out carol singing with us," Gary Roberts said, grinning.

"Don't count on it," Jill Redfern replied.

"*Peace on earth, and mercy mild,*" Mandy sang. She gave Jill a dig in the ribs and Jill joined in.

"*God and sinners reconciled,*" the carollers roared.

Blackie scampered over to where Pandora was sitting behind her owner. The Pekinese was watching the carol singers and joining

in now and again with short, sharp yelps. Blackie gave Pandora a nudge with his nose and Pandora yelped even more.

Mrs Ponsonby turned. "Blackie!" she thundered. The Labrador took off and streaked under a chair.

James made a dive for Blackie as Mrs Ponsonby scooped Pandora up and clasped her pet to her chest.

"Sorry, Mrs Ponsonby," James apologised, as the carol singing drifted to a stop.

"Really, James," Mrs Ponsonby scolded. "If you can't keep that dog of yours under control, you shouldn't bring him to rehearsals. Oh, my poor darling," Mrs Ponsonby murmured to Pandora. "Did wicked Blackie upset you?"

Pandora sneezed, jumped out of Mrs Ponsonby's arms and raced off behind the piano. Sandy scampered after her and Mrs Ponsonby let out a screech.

"Pandora must *not* be overexcited," she declared. "My little angel is so highly strung."

"Whoops!" said Peter Foster as Timmy shot off after the other dogs. Peter made a lunge for his pet but Timmy managed to slip out of his grasp. The dogs had clearly had enough carol singing for the day; they wanted to play. In no time at all they were rolling around and chasing one another.

"Look at them!" said Max, delightedly. "They're having a great time."

"They're leading my precious Pandora astray," Mrs Ponsonby wailed, as she waded into the midst of the dogs, scattering them in all directions. Blackie bumped into a chair and it fell over, spilling song sheets on the floor.

"What a noise!" a voice said from the door. "I thought Mrs Ponsonby was in charge of you all."

Mandy swung round. Mrs Trigg stood there, looking very disapproving. Mandy looked at her watch; it must be time to go. Mrs Trigg had insisted on coming to collect Max. She took the responsibility of looking after him very seriously and always seemed worried in case anything should happen to him while he was in her care.

"I *am* in charge, Maggie," Mrs Ponsonby declared, coming out from behind the piano. Her face was as red as the pompom on her hat. She had been chasing after Pandora. At that moment, Pandora scampered up to her and Mrs Ponsonby bent down and picked up her pet. Carol sheets were scattered on the floor and several more chairs had been overturned.

Max wrestled a rather chewed sheet of music from Sandy, and handed it back to Mrs Ponsonby. "Sorry, Mrs Ponsonby," he said.

Mrs Ponsonby took the soggy piece of

paper. "Don't worry about it, my dear! We've got plenty." The carollers cheerfully carried on tidying up.

Mrs Trigg looked around and sniffed. "Animals!" she said. "What a mess they cause!"

Sandy gave a short bark and shot across the room to Mrs Trigg, wagging his tail furiously. No matter what Mrs Trigg thought of Sandy, the little dog loved *her*.

"Hmmph!" said Mrs Trigg as Sandy sat down almost on top of her boots and thumped his stumpy tail. "I see *you've* been naughty, too," she said sternly, looking down at the little dog. But Mandy noticed that she bent down to give him a quick pat.

Mrs Trigg shook her head at Mrs Ponsonby. "It seems to me that pets are nothing but trouble," she announced.

Mrs Ponsonby drew herself up. "I can't agree with you, Maggie," she declared. "Pandora is very well-behaved – usually. And she is such a good companion to me. I wouldn't be without her for the world. I'm never lonely with my Pandora around."

Pandora settled down in Mrs Ponsonby's arms, rubbing her head against her owner's hand.

Mrs Trigg looked at the little dog. "Well, there is that," she agreed. "Sometimes I do get lonely," she added softly.

"Then you really should think about having a pet, Maggie," Mrs Ponsonby said briskly. "You'd never feel alone if you had a little dog like my Pandora to keep you company. Didn't I see you walking Sandy this morning?"

Mrs Trigg flushed. "Max was at school," she explained. "Sandy needed a walk."

"That's another thing about dogs," Mrs Ponsonby continued. "They get you out of the house – you would meet people. You spend far too much time cleaning that cottage of yours, my dear. Why don't you come back to the WI? You used to enjoy it so much and you need to get out more!"

With that, Mrs Ponsonby turned away and began to shepherd the children into their coats and hats.

Mrs Trigg looked after her. "Well, really!"

she said, her face rather red.

Mandy came to stand beside Mrs Trigg. "Mrs Ponsonby bosses *everybody* around," she said sympathetically. "But she's right about one thing, Mrs Trigg. Pets can be wonderful company."

"Hmmph!" said Mrs Trigg. "They can also be a lot of hard work. Come along, Max."

Mandy watched as Mrs Trigg bustled Max and Sandy out of the door. Mrs Trigg might have taken Sandy for a walk, but that didn't mean she liked dogs. It wasn't going to be easy changing Mrs Trigg's mind about pets!

4

An abandoned puppy

"I think it's going to snow again," Mr Hope said on Saturday morning, as he came into the residential unit at Animal Ark. It had snowed a lot in the last few days. The snow lay deep and thick on the moors around Welford and there were drifts piled high against the hedges in some of the lanes. Even the village green was totally white, and the

41

branches of the surrounding trees were covered in snow.

It was so cold, Mandy had found icicles hanging outside her bedroom window that morning. She had hurried downstairs to put out fresh nuts and bacon rind for the birds; it wasn't easy for them to find food with this much snow around. There would certainly be enough snow for sledging, as long as there wasn't a sudden thaw.

"I hope it snows all day and all night," she said happily. "We're planning to go sledging tomorrow." She had a tiny kitten in her arms. It had swallowed a plastic bottle top, which had lodged in the young animal's throat. Mr Hope had needed to put the kitten to sleep before he could remove it.

"I love sledging," said James, who had arrived after breakfast. "When is Max coming over, Mandy?"

Mandy put the kitten back in its cage. "Any time now," she replied, tickling the little animal under its chin. "He's coming to help choose the Christmas tree. Since he can't have one at Holly Cottage, I thought

he could help decorate ours." It was now the Christmas holidays – time to put up the Animal Ark Christmas tree!

"I saw Max's gran out walking Sandy again yesterday," Mr Hope said. "She seemed to be getting on really well with him – much better than she was earlier in the week."

Mandy smiled. "She's been taking him for walks while Max has been at school," she told her father. "She won't have to do that over the Christmas holidays, of course."

Adam Hope put his head on one side,

looking thoughtful. "Mmm," he said. "Pity. She looked as if she was quite enjoying it."

"Mrs Ponsonby told her she should get a dog," Mandy said.

Mr Hope laughed. "It isn't often you and Mrs Ponsonby agree on anything!"

"Oh, but I think *everybody* should have animals in their life," Mandy declared. "Just look at Max and Sandy."

Max and Sandy had been regular visitors to Animal Ark over the last few days. Max loved seeing the animals and Sandy had made firm friends with Blackie.

"We should get this little fellow home in time for Christmas," Adam Hope remarked, looking at the kitten.

Mandy bent down and smiled at the kitten. "No more bottle tops," she warned. She glanced round the other cages. Only the gerbil and the hamster remained now; the other animals had all gone back to their owners. Mandy was always glad to see animals get well enough to go home, but she missed them when they left.

"I've rung George Fenton," Mr Hope

went on. "He says you can go and choose a tree any time, and I'll pay for it next time I'm passing."

Mr Fenton was Amy's dad. He owned a sawmill just on the edge of the village, and at Christmas he turned his workshop into a Christmas-tree shop.

"Can I choose a really big one, Dad?" Mandy asked.

Emily Hope, Mandy's mum, came through the door just as Mandy was speaking. "Just make sure it'll fit in the living-room," she said, her green eyes twinkling. "We don't want to have to chop the top off."

"I've measured it," Mandy replied. "We can get a two-metre one and still have room to put the star on top!"

"Wow!" said Mrs Hope. "It's just as well you've got Paddy to help bring that home."

Mandy grinned. "We're going to take my sledge," she told her mother. "Paul has been practising with Paddy. He says his pony just loves pulling a sledge – and he's very strong."

"There's Max!" James called, looking out

of the window. "Let's go, Mandy."

Mandy glanced outside. The garden was already carpeted in fresh snow. The snowman that she, James and Max had made yesterday stood in the middle of the lawn. There was a covering of snow on the carrot they had used for a nose.

"Wrap up warmly," Mrs Hope called after them as they raced out of the residential unit.

Mandy and James shrugged themselves into heavy jackets, crammed woolly hats on their heads, and thrust their hands into gloves. Blackie rushed out from behind the reception desk to meet them.

"Thanks for looking after him," James said to Jean Knox, the receptionist. Blackie wasn't allowed into the residential unit with the sick animals.

Jean looked over her spectacles at James. "Any time, James," she replied. "He's good company."

Mandy put her head on one side. "I wish Mrs Trigg thought dogs were good company," she said.

"Oh, knowing you, Mandy, you'll persuade her." Jean laughed, nodding her head. Her glasses slid off her nose and bounced on the end of their chain.

"Maybe I will," Mandy said thoughtfully. "You know, she's still letting Sandy sleep in the kitchen because it's been snowing so much. She says she can mop the floor every day."

"That's a lot better than the potting shed for Sandy," Jean agreed.

Mandy opened the door and Sandy threw himself at her. She bent down to let him lick her face in welcome. Blackie bounded out of the door, and the two dogs rolled on the ground, chasing each other and kicking up great flurries of soft, powdery snow.

"Christmas-tree time!" Max said happily.

Mandy smiled. She was *really* glad she had suggested that Max help choose the tree. He seemed so excited about decorating it.

"Here, Blackie," she called, clipping on Blackie's lead as the Labrador bounded up to her.

"I've got the sledge," James called, dragging a red sledge out of the porch. "Let's go!"

First they had to go and collect Paul and Paddy from Paul's house. They roped the sledge to the harness they had rigged up for Paddy. Blackie gave a short bark and leaped on to the sledge. Sandy followed, jumping on behind the Labrador.

Paul grinned as James tried to shoo the dogs off. "Leave them," he said. "It's good practice for Paddy."

As they walked down the main street they made quite a picture. Mr and Mrs McFarlane came out of the post office to watch.

"Are you playing Santa Claus?" Mr McFarlane called to them.

"Paddy makes a good Rudolph, but where's his red nose?" Mrs McFarlane joked.

They laughed and waved. As they passed the Fox and Goose, the landlord, Mr Hardy, came out to watch. "You need some jingle bells," he remarked, smiling.

Mandy looked at Paddy. The sturdy little Exmoor pony really was enjoying pulling the sledge.

Paul had got Paddy from a rescue sanctuary. The little pony had been very badly treated. The first time Mandy saw him, he had been in such poor condition that he wouldn't even have been able to pull a sledge. Now his coat was a glossy greyish brown and his eyes were clear and bright – not sad, the way they had been when Mandy first saw him at the sanctuary.

As Mandy watched, Paddy's head went

up and he shook his dark-brown mane, his breath cloudy on the frosty air. Paul had done a wonderful job with Paddy — and Paddy had loved Paul right from the start.

Mandy laid a hand on Paddy's warm winter coat. "Good boy, Paddy!" she said softly. "Good boy!"

Soon they were out of the village and heading towards the sawmill.

Mandy saw Amy perched on the gate as they turned into the driveway. She stood up, clutching the gate with one mittened hand and waving to them with the other. The bright yellow bobbles on her woolly hat danced merrily as she called out to them. "I've told Dad to show you all the best trees," she told them, swinging the gate open.

Paddy plodded through the gate into the yard and Mr Fenton came out of the shed. "Come on, you lot," he called. "Let's go and choose your tree. Then you can have some mince-pies while I rope it on to the sledge for you."

Mandy and the others followed him excitedly into the shed. The smell of resin and pine needles filled the space. Mandy gazed at the forest of trees propped up against the walls. There were so many to choose from, and each one they looked at seemed better than the last.

Finally, the perfect tree was chosen. "That one!" Max said, pointing to a large, glossy fir tree. The branches of the tree he had selected were feathery and full. Best of all, it had a long, straight top branch.

"Perfect for the Christmas star," Mandy said, smiling happily.

James and Paul nodded in agreement.

"Good choice, Max," James said as he waved to Mr Fenton.

Mandy looked at Max's shining face. He might not have a tree at Holly Cottage, but choosing the one for Animal Ark was surely the next best thing!

"Amy's mum's mince-pies were great," James said as they slowly made their way back down the lane towards Animal Ark.

Mandy laughed. "She promised to have some more ready for us when we go carol singing," she said.

Paul was leading Paddy, guiding the pony carefully over the rough track. Mandy looked up as a large snowflake settled on her nose. "Dad was right!" she exclaimed. "He said it would snow again."

"I wonder if the pool at the bottom of Beacon Hill will be frozen," James said.

"Where's that?" asked Max.

Mandy pointed across the fields to a snow-topped hill. "Over there," she said. "It's a great hill for sledging, and sometimes, if it's really cold, the pool at the bottom freezes over and we can skate on it."

"You have to be careful, though," Paul warned. "The pool is part of the river and the ice has to be really, *really* solid before you try skating."

"Sledging will be enough for me," Max said happily. "You know, Welford is a really great place. We've got a park near where I live, but nothing like this. It must be great living in the country all the time."

Mandy smiled and lifted her face to the snowflakes. "It is," she agreed. "I can't imagine living anywhere else but Welford."

Paddy's hooves were beginning to make marks in the newly fallen snow, and the sledge ran smoothly over the snowy ground. The tree, securely roped on, brushed its branches against Mandy's legs as she walked and the two dogs started chasing snowflakes. If the snow kept up, it was going to be a perfect Christmas.

They turned out of the track on to the back road that ran between the Fentons' sawmill and Welford. Suddenly Sandy stopped at the edge of the ditch that bordered the road. Hanging over the ditch was a bushy bramble, heavy with snow.

"Watch the bramble doesn't prick you, Sandy," Max warned.

Sandy turned his head towards his young master but wouldn't come away from the ditch. He stood there, legs stiff, tail erect, sniffing and growling softly.

"Come on, Sandy," Max said.

But the little dog stayed where he was,

and began to bark urgently.

Max frowned. "What is it, boy?" he asked.

Sandy looked up at him, still barking.

Max gazed down into the ditch. Then he reached out a gloved hand and moved a branch aside. "Oh, no!" he cried out. "Come and look at this."

Mandy hurried over, alerted by the note of shock in Max's voice. "What is it?" she asked. Then she saw for herself, and her heart began to beat faster.

There, lying huddled in the ditch beneath the bramble-bush, was a little puppy. Its coat was dark, but it was fast being covered with snow. And it wasn't moving.

Mandy felt her breath come back in a rush. Then she scrambled down into the ditch and lifted the puppy carefully. She breathed a sigh of relief as, through her gloves, she felt some warmth coming from the puppy's small body. It was alive.

But then Mandy caught sight of the snow where the puppy had lain. She gasped. It was red with blood. There was more blood on her gloves.

She called to the others. "It's a puppy. It's alive — but it's hurt. Bleeding. We've got to get it to Animal Ark as quickly as possible!"

James reached down and took the puppy gently from her. Mandy scrambled out of the ditch, unwrapping her scarf from her neck. "Here," she said. "Wrap this round it. We've got to keep it warm. The poor little thing looks as if it's been there a long time. It's unconscious."

As Mandy muffled the puppy up in her scarf, the little animal opened its eyes and let out a weak cry.

"Oh, the poor little thing," Max said. "It must be in real pain."

Mandy nodded. "The sooner we get back to Animal Ark, the better."

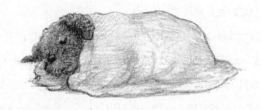

5

Safe at Animal Ark

Mandy gazed anxiously at the little puppy as it lay on the examination table at Animal Ark. "How is it?" she asked her mother.

Emily Hope smiled as she finished cleaning the wound on the puppy's leg. "It's a *she*," she said. "I think she's going to be all right. She looks worse than she is, with the fur shaved off around her wound, but it will soon grow back. She's in shock and badly bruised, too, but you got to her just in time, Mandy. Another fifteen minutes in that ditch and she would have died from the cold."

"It was Sandy that found her," Mandy told her mother.

Mrs Hope looked at Max's worried face as he stood on the other side of the examination table. "Then Sandy is a very clever puppy," she said. "Let's go and congratulate him."

Mrs Hope settled the injured puppy comfortably in one of the cages in the residential unit, with a warm blanket tucked round her. "There," she said. "A good sleep and she'll be as right as rain – except for her leg. We'll have to keep an eye on that."

"She won't be lame, will she?" James asked.

Emily Hope shook her head. "It isn't as bad as that," she assured him. "She should be ready to leave us in a few days."

"But she hasn't got a home," Mandy said. "She doesn't even have a collar. And she's so tiny. How old is she, Mum?"

"About five months," Mrs Hope replied. "I'll be able to examine her better tomorrow, but I'd say she's probably had all her injections."

"How do you think she got into the ditch, Mrs Hope?" James asked.

Mandy's mum looked serious. "I think she was abandoned," she said. "It happens sometimes. People get a puppy and forget that they are a lot of work. Then they take them out into the country and just let them go."

"But she was *hurt*," Mandy protested.

Mrs Hope looked sympathetically at Mandy. "Sometimes people just throw the pup out of a moving car," she explained. "It's a terrible thing to do, but at least this little puppy has been saved – thanks to you lot."

Mandy shook her head. *How could anyone be so cruel?* "Oh, I promised I'd phone Paul," she said. "He had to take Paddy home and he's really worried about the puppy."

"You do that," Mrs Hope said. "Then we can cheer ourselves up by decorating the Christmas tree."

Max's face lit up. "Can I stay and help?" he asked.

Mandy turned to him as they went out of the door. "Of course you can," she declared. "You're the chief tree decorator this year!"

Blackie and Sandy bounded over to them as they went into the reception area. Max grinned and bent down to give Sandy a cuddle. "And you're a hero, Sandy," he said.

Blackie gave a short bark. "See," said James. "Blackie thinks so as well."

"I wonder if Holly will like the tree," Max said.

"Holly?" asked Mrs Hope.

Max blushed. "Oh, that's what I was calling the puppy we rescued — just to myself. It's sort of Christmassy, don't you think?"

"I think Holly's a great name," Mandy agreed, when she came back from making her phone call to Paul. She turned to her mother. "What will happen to her?" she asked.

"She'll have to go to the RSPCA once she's better," Mrs Hope replied. "It should only be a few days — Christmas Eve at the latest."

Mandy frowned. "But then nobody would be able to adopt her until after Christmas, Mum," she said. "You know how many puppies are abandoned then. It will be really hard for them to find her a home."

Emily Hope sighed. "I know," she said. "But what else can we do? I can't send her to the RSPCA until her leg is better. They have such a lot of work already and, besides, they wouldn't allow anyone to adopt her until her leg had healed."

Mandy raised her head. "*We* could find her a home," she said. "We could find somebody here in Welford to take her."

Mrs Hope laughed. "I wouldn't put it past you, Mandy," she said. "Now, how about putting up that Christmas tree before Holly wakes up?"

Mandy, James and Max quickly set to work covering the tub for the tree with some bright Christmas paper.

Mr Hope arrived just as they finished. He had been out visiting one of the local farms and his beard was dusted with snow. "It's snowing again," he said, moving towards the fire. "It's freezing out there."

"Do you think it's cold enough for the pool at the bottom of Beacon Hill to ice over?" James asked.

"I should imagine so," Adam Hope replied.

But Mandy wasn't thinking of ice-skating.

She plunged straight into their story about Holly, dragging her father into the residential unit to see the puppy. Adam Hope bent down to look at the sleeping pup. Holly was curled up, cosy and warm in her blanket. She was fast asleep, her nose twitching. Now and again she made soft snuffling noises.

"What breed is she, Dad?" Mandy whispered.

"She looks like some sort of terrier-cross to me," Mr Hope replied. "A pretty little thing," he added, smiling. "Terriers – especially cross-breeds – are tough little things. No wonder Holly survived her ordeal."

"Well, she's safe now," Mandy breathed. "With people who will be kind to her," she added.

Adam Hope ruffled his daughter's hair. "Come on," he said. "Let's leave her to sleep. We can bring her out later to see the Christmas tree."

"Oh, isn't it beautiful!" Mandy exclaimed,

gazing at the Christmas tree. The dark-green branches shimmered in the firelight, giving out a wonderful scent in the heat of the room.

"It'll look even more beautiful when it's decorated," Mrs Hope said, coming into the room with a huge cardboard box in her hands. Blackie and Sandy followed at her heels. The dogs had been banned from the living-room while Mr Hope was putting up the tree. Now they stopped, side by side, and looked at the tree, sniffing the fircones. Sandy launched himself at the tree and Max made a leap for him.

"Leave him," said Mr Hope.

Max drew back, puzzled. Sandy rushed at the tree. As the prickly branches caught his nose, he jumped back, his head low. Cautiously he moved forward again, testing the needles on the branches. Then he sneezed.

"I think he'll keep his distance now," Mrs Hope laughed.

Max laughed too. "This is Sandy's first Christmas," he said.

"So let's make it a really good one," Mandy announced, rummaging in the decorations box. "Look! I've found the star for the top of the tree!"

Half an hour later, Mr Hope moved the stepladder away from the tree. Outside, the afternoon had grown dark. The light from the log fire lit up the glittering baubles of glass, the sparkly tinsel and the gold-wrapped candy sticks hanging from the tree's branches. Mr Hope plugged in the fairy lights. "Who's going to switch them on, then?" he asked.

Mandy spun round, a wide smile on her lips. "Max," she said.

Max walked slowly over to the switch and pressed it down. The tiny white bulbs sprang into life, dancing on the shiny decorations and glowing against the darkness outside.

"Wow!" said James. "That is just the *best* tree ever!"

Sandy and Blackie crept closer to the tree, lying down under it and gazing up at the twinkling lights.

"Now it *really* feels like Christmas,"

Mandy said, smiling happily.

"And I smell mince-pies," James added.

Everybody laughed. "Trust James!" said Mrs Hope. "Come on, you lot; you deserve a treat after all your hard work. Mince-pies all round."

6

Sandy in danger

"Holly is looking much better today," Mrs Hope told Mandy next day as she examined the little pup.

"Isn't she beautiful?" Mandy said, as Holly looked up at Mrs Hope and gave her hand a trusting lick. The puppy's little face looked adorable. "Why on earth would anyone abandon her? She's perfect."

"Who knows?" said her mother. "The important thing is that she's a fine, healthy pup and her leg will soon be better."

"When do you think her bandage can come off, Mum?" Mandy asked.

"Tomorrow," Mrs Hope told her. "The wound wasn't very deep and it's healing nicely."

"But we don't have to send her away yet, do we?" Mandy asked.

Mrs Hope shook her head. "I'd like to keep her for a few more days, just to make sure she isn't suffering from delayed shock. She's still very young and she must have had quite a fright."

Mandy frowned. "But it'll be Christmas in three days' time," she said.

"Don't worry," Mrs Hope said. "We won't put her out in the snow."

Mandy smiled. "Oh, I know *that*, Mum," she said. She looked out of the window. "James and Max and I are going sledging on Beacon Hill this morning."

Mrs Hope rose from the table. "I wish I

could come with you. It's years since I've been sledging."

"Why don't you?" Mandy asked.

Mrs Hope smiled. "Because I've got patients to see," she said. "Now, remember: wrap up "

"Warmly," Mandy finished, grinning. "We will."

"Shh!" said Max to Mandy and James when they arrived at Holly Cottage. He was smiling.

"What is it?" whispered James.

Max put a finger to his lips and led them towards the living-room door. It was open slightly and Mandy and James peered into the room. Mrs Trigg was sitting on the sofa in front of the fire, dozing – and beside her, curled up at her side, was Sandy.

"What is she going to say when she wakes up?" Mandy whispered, grinning.

Max shook his head. "Gran said Sandy could come into the living-room because the weather was so cold," he explained.

"So she's getting to like him?" James asked.

"She won't admit it," Max said. "But I think she is. Only I don't know what she's going to say if she wakes and finds that Sandy has crept up to sit beside her – on the sofa!"

Just at that moment a log shifted in the fire and Mrs Trigg stirred. Her hand went out and touched Sandy's neck. Sandy lifted his head and licked her hand.

Mrs Trigg's eyes flew open and she looked down at the little dog. "Well, really, Sandy!" she said sternly. "Get down at once."

Sandy looked up at her and snuggled closer, clearly delighted at having sneaked up beside Mrs Trigg. Mandy watched in amazement as the old lady's mouth curved in a reluctant smile.

"Bad dog," Mrs Trigg said. But this time she didn't say it as if she meant it. She stood up and brushed her hands down her apron. "Look what you've done, Sandy," she scolded. "Now I've got dog hairs on my apron."

Sandy jumped down off the sofa and wagged his tail, then he rubbed his head against Mrs Trigg's ankles and nibbled at her shoe laces.

"Silly little dog," Mrs Trigg said, bending down and giving him a pat. "Shoo! I've got work to do."

Mandy, James and Max looked at one another. Maybe Sandy was winning Mrs Trigg round after all!

The sun was shining on the crisp, white snow as Mandy, James and Max made their way to Beacon Hill. Mandy looked at the

71

pool at the foot of the hill. "We could try skating another day," she said. "The ice looks firm enough."

Blackie gave a short bark and raced on ahead towards the pool.

Sandy followed, overtaking Blackie and rolling in the snow in front of him. The two dogs leaped and rolled together. They were having a great time.

"They love playing together, don't they?" Max said.

James smiled. "The best of friends," he agreed as Blackie dived into a snowdrift and started kicking up enormous clouds of snow.

Sandy scampered out of range, waiting for his chum to reappear out of the snowdrift. As Mandy watched, she saw Sandy go very still and turn towards the pool, as if he had just heard something.

Mandy looked across the shining sheet of ice but couldn't see anything. "What's Sandy doing?" she asked Max.

Max shrugged. "Maybe he heard a bird or a rabbit," he said.

Mandy nodded. "Oh, look at Blackie!" She giggled.

Blackie burst out of the snowdrift, shaking snow in great dollops from his coat.

"It's a snowstorm!" James yelled.

Blackie barked and began to race past Sandy, towards the frozen pool beyond.

As Blackie ran towards the pool, Sandy turned and gave chase, running at Blackie and growling. The Labrador steered clear of him, keeping away from the pool.

Max frowned. "What on earth is Sandy doing?" he asked. "He's never done that before!"

Blackie ran towards the terrier again, trying to get round him, but Sandy stood his ground, his teeth bared.

"Sandy!" Max called. "Stop that!"

James ran ahead and grasped Blackie's collar. At once Sandy relaxed, coming to Max and wagging his tail.

"What was all that about?" Max asked, puzzled. "They usually get on so well together."

James shrugged. "Sandy seems all right

now," he said. "Come on, let's go sledging."

They trudged up to the top of the hill.

"Race you to the bottom!" James yelled, pushing his sledge off from the top of Beacon Hill.

"That's not fair – you've got a head start," Mandy called after him as she pushed her own sledge off.

The snow was deep and soft. Mandy's sledge skimmed over it, sending up flurries of powdery snow as she went. The sky was a clear blue and, below, the frozen pool was silver in the winter sun.

"Wait for me," called Max behind her.

Mandy turned to watch as Max launched himself down the slope. When she turned back she shouted, "James! Get out of the way!"

James, in front of her, turned round briefly as Mandy's sledge shot down the hill. But he was too late; Mandy was going to crash into him. James turned his sledge wildly, trying to get out of her path. Blackie bounded past downhill with Sandy at his heels. The dogs were having a wonderful time.

"Uh-oh!" Mandy said, dragging on the ropes of her sledge as she hurtled towards James.

Max took a wide sweep to avoid them both. "See you at the bottom," he called, as Mandy's sledge crashed into James's. The two sledges overturned, tipping Mandy and James out into the snow. Mandy sat up, laughing, as James dived head first into a snowdrift.

"Are you all right?" she spluttered.

James's head appeared, covered in snow. He clambered back on to his sledge. "I'll still race you!" he said.

But Mandy wasn't listening. Down near the pool at the bottom of the hill Sandy was barking furiously. "Look!" Mandy exclaimed. "Sandy is acting oddly again."

As Max's sledge made its way downhill, the little dog ran up to meet it, running right in its path. Max turned his sledge, desperately trying to avoid Sandy. For a few moments his sledge ran along the side of the hill and Sandy slowed down.

Max steered his sledge downwards again.

But again Sandy ran in front of him, barking furiously.

The ice on the pool gleamed in the sunshine. As they watched, Max once more turned his sledge sharply to avoid Sandy. This time the sledge overturned and he fell out on to the snow. But Sandy was going too fast to stop. The little dog skidded on the edge of the ice and shot out on to the surface of the pool, scrabbling widely to keep his balance.

"On, no!" Mandy cried. "Look, James!" The ice beneath Sandy was beginning to crack up.

Sandy scrabbled desperately for a footing on the slippery surface. Max got up and began to race towards his pet.

"No, Max! Wait!" James yelled. "The ice is cracking!"

Mandy and James pushed their sledges off, racing downhill. Mandy got there first and grabbed Max. "You can't go out there," she gasped. "The ice won't take your weight. We could see cracks all over the pool from further up the hill."

Max's face was white. "But what about Sandy?" he asked. "If the ice gives way, he'll drown!"

7

Rescue!

"What are we going to do?" James asked. Blackie strained forwards; he wanted to help Sandy. James kept a tight hold on his collar.

Mandy frowned, thinking hard. Then an idea came to her. "We've got the sledges," she said. "We can lay one of them down at the edge of the ice where it's thickest. It would be like a platform. And the sledges are plastic; they aren't heavy."

"I think mine is even lighter than yours, Mandy," James said.

"That's it then," said Max. "If you two hold on to the sledge, I can crawl out and try to reach Sandy."

"You?" Mandy sounded surprised.

Max looked at her seriously. "Sandy *is* my dog," he said.

Mandy glanced quickly at the puppy out on the ice. He was about two metres from the bank; cracks were spreading out around him. There was no time to lose and no time to argue.

"Right," she said. "You go on, Max. We'll pull the sledge in if the ice cracks under you."

"Stay, Blackie!" James ordered.

The Labrador looked up at him worriedly, but didn't move even when James let go of his collar.

Quickly, Mandy and James laid James's sledge down on the ice at the edge of the pool and Max began to crawl along the makeshift platform. The ice groaned under him and Mandy held her breath, watching the boy edge out towards his pet. She and James hung on tightly to the end of the sledge. There was a sudden snap as a large piece of ice further out broke loose and turned on its side. It floated for a moment before breaking up.

"That water will be really cold," James said worriedly.

Mandy nodded and bent down, ready to pull in the sledge if necessary.

Max looked back. "I don't know if I can reach him," he said.

Mandy watched while Max inched his way along the sledge as far as he could go. He was as close to Sandy as he could get now.

Sandy was gazing at Max, but Max couldn't reach him. Even with his arms outstretched, Sandy was still about twenty centimetres away from Max. Max stretched out a hand. "Come on, Sandy," he coaxed. "Jump for it. Jump on to the sledge."

There was another groan and then a loud crack. Mandy saw the ice under Sandy crack right across. Sandy's paws scrabbled at the ice under him as it split from side to side, leaving a great, gaping hole. Then he lost his balance, tumbling into the water. Max made a lunge and the breath stopped in Mandy's throat as the sledge wobbled on the very edge of the ice hole.

"Max!" she yelled.

But Max wasn't listening; Sandy had disappeared beneath the water. There was a flurry and the little dog appeared, struggling to stay afloat.

Blackie made to rush forward on to the

ice but James caught his collar. "No, boy," he said. "I know you want to help, but we can't have two of you out there."

"Don't let him sink under the ice," Mandy muttered, her eyes on Sandy. "He'd be trapped. Swim, Sandy, swim!"

As if he heard her, Sandy started to doggy-paddle towards Max. Another raft of ice floated towards him, grazing his side, pushing him further away from Max and forcing him underwater.

Max made a final grab, plunging his hand into the water as Sandy disappeared again. Then, with a heave, Max pulled Sandy free and hauled him up on to the sledge. At once, James and Mandy gently started to pull the sledge back until it rested at the edge of the pool. Max clambered off with Sandy in his arms.

"You did it, Max," James said.

But Max's expression was worried. "He's so cold. We'll have to get him back as quickly as we can."

Mandy unzipped her anorak. "Yours is wet, Max," she explained. "But mine is dry.

Sandy will be warm tucked up in here."

Max put Sandy gently into Mandy's arms and she zipped her fleecy anorak up around him. "There," she said to the shivering little dog. "Now we have to get you back to Animal Ark as quickly as possible."

Mr Hope was in the surgery when they arrived. Jean Knox rang through to him at once, then she bundled the children and dogs into the warmth of the living-room. A fire blazed cheerfully in the grate and the Christmas tree lights were on, but Mandy was too worried to admire them.

They laid Sandy down in front of the fire. The little animal was still shaking with cold, but not quite as much as he had been. Jean brought two big fluffy towels – one for Sandy and one for Max.

"Get that wet anorak off," she said to Max. "You're shivering. Mandy can rub Sandy down while I get her a dry jumper."

Mandy wrapped one of the towels round the little dog, rubbing the warmth back into him, while Max took off his anorak.

Underneath, his jumper was also wet.

"I'll get you one of Mandy's," said briskly, going out of the door. "And I've phoned your gran. She's coming right over."

Mandy finished rubbing Sandy down and changed into a dry jumper. The one she had been wearing was wet all down the front where Sandy had snuggled close to her. Blackie curled up beside Sandy.

"Good boy, Blackie," she murmured to the Labrador. "You're helping to keep him warm too."

Max dried himself off and slipped on the jumper that Jean brought for him.

"Your dad is just coming," Jean said to Mandy. "What on earth happened?"

At that moment Mr Hope came in, and Mandy explained while her father examined the puppy.

"Well," he said, standing up. "The little fellow seems none the worse for his adventure. You three seem to be turning into a Welford Dog Rescue Team. That's the second pup you've rescued in the last few days!" He looked serious suddenly. "But, you know, that was a very dangerous thing to do, Max."

"It certainly was," added a voice from the door.

Mandy looked round. Mrs Trigg was standing there in her black coat and hat. Her face was white with worry and she looked angry. "What on earth were you thinking of, Max? You might have been drowned – and all for the sake of that dog. I might have known – animals are nothing but trouble! He'll have to go!" she declared.

Mandy's heart sank. Mrs Trigg had been growing fond of Sandy, she was sure of it. Now she seemed to hate him more than ever.

Max looked dumbly at his grandmother, the tears standing in his eyes. Mandy felt suddenly angry. It was so unfair! She could understand how worried and upset Mrs Trigg was, but she had got it all wrong.

"That isn't true, Mrs Trigg," she burst out. "Sandy was trying to *help* Max."

Mrs Trigg looked down her nose at

Mandy. "Help?" she said. "You call getting itself half drowned and putting Max in danger *helping*?"

"No," said Mandy. "You don't understand. Sandy knew the ice was thin; James and Max will tell you." She turned to the boys. "Remember how Sandy warned Blackie off the ice? He growled and bared his teeth."

"That's right," agreed James. "He had never behaved like that before. We wondered what was wrong."

"Nonsense," Mrs Trigg said.

"Maybe not, Mrs Trigg," Mr Hope cut in. "Dogs have a very keen sense of hearing. If Sandy had heard the ice creaking and beginning to break up, he might have known instinctively that there was danger out there. Go on, Mandy; tell us exactly what Sandy did."

Mandy took a deep breath. "When Max came downhill on his sledge he was heading towards the pool," she explained. "Sandy kept running in front of him, trying to make him change course. Max lost control of his sledge and it tipped over and he fell out, but Sandy couldn't stop so he ended up out on the ice. If it hadn't been for Sandy, *Max* would have slid right out on to the ice."

She turned to Mrs Trigg, looking pleadingly up at her. "So you see, Mrs Trigg, Sandy saved Max's life. You can't send him away. Anybody can see how much Sandy loves Max, and Max loves Sandy just as much! Max is missing his mum and dad such a lot, and Sandy is his friend. You *can't* take him away from Max – especially not at Christmas time!"

Mandy stopped, afraid she had gone too far. Mrs Trigg looked at her for a long moment. Then the old lady looked away, her eyes going round the room. She gazed at the shining Christmas tree in the window, then her eyes rested on Max and Sandy. Max was sitting in front of the fire with Sandy in his arms. The firelight cast a rosy glow over both of them.

"They certainly seem to love each other," Mrs Trigg said softly to Mandy. She smiled and went on in a low voice, "It's so

Christmassy in here. I remember when my husband was alive we used to have such good Christmases. Oh, how he loved it. He would decorate the cottage from top to bottom and I would bake a Christmas cake – and mince-pies, and brandy-snaps and Yule logs. Oh, everything! I haven't bothered about Christmas much since Bill died. Max's mum and dad haven't been able to come for Christmas in recent years, so it hasn't seemed worth it just for myself."

"But it *isn't* just yourself this year, Mrs Trigg," Mandy said gently.

Mrs Trigg looked at her in surprise. "You know, you're right, Mandy," she said. "My cottage isn't very Christmassy. Maybe I should do something about that, my dear."

Mandy smiled at the old lady. She wasn't angry after all.

Then Mrs Trigg spoke briskly. "Let's get you home, Max," she said. "Sandy, too. It seems that I owe him an apology. Perhaps he could sit with us in the living-room from now on – but not on the furniture."

Max's face lit up. "Can he lie on the rug in front of the fire? He's had such a shock today. He nearly drowned."

"I think that would be all right," said his grandmother. "Come along now."

"Can I go and see Holly first?" Max asked.

"Holly?" said Mrs Trigg.

Max nodded. "It's a puppy that Sandy found," he explained. "The poor little thing was abandoned. She would have frozen to death if it hadn't been for Sandy."

Mrs Trigg smiled. "It seems I've got a lot to learn about Sandy," she said.

"Would *you* like to see Holly, Mrs Trigg?" Mandy asked.

Mrs Trigg looked surprised. "Me?" she said. "Why would I want to see a puppy?"

Mandy smiled. "Oh, you might like her," she suggested, with a grin.

Mrs Trigg looked round the eager faces of the children. "I suppose I might as well have a look," she said after a moment. "After all, what harm can it do?"

Mandy's smile got even wider. "None at all, Mrs Trigg," she said. "None at all."

8

Mrs Trigg's surprise

Mrs Trigg followed the others into the residential unit. Mandy unhooked Holly's cage and lifted her out. "How are you?" she whispered, cuddling the little puppy.

Holly looked up at her and licked her nose. Mandy giggled.

"We've brought somebody new to see

you," James said. "Say hello to Mrs Trigg, Holly."

Mandy held the puppy out to the old woman. Mrs Trigg took a step back. "Oh, I don't think I could," she said.

"She's very gentle, Gran," Max assured his grandmother.

Mrs Trigg held out her arms slowly and Mandy put the puppy into them. Holly snuggled down and closed her eyes.

"She'll soon be as good as new," Mandy said.

Mrs Trigg stood quite still, looking at Holly. She was holding the puppy a little awkwardly, but Holly didn't seem to mind. Holly opened her eyes for a moment and nibbled at the old lady's fingers. Mandy tickled the puppy under the chin. "She likes you doing that," she said to Mrs Trigg.

Mrs Trigg put a finger under Holly's chin. The puppy looked up at her with big melting eyes and yawned.

"Isn't she adorable?" Max said.

"What exactly happened to her?" Mrs Trigg asked, looking at Holly's bandage.

Mandy laid her hand lightly on Holly's leg. "Holly was abandoned," she explained. "Mum thinks she was thrown out of a moving car."

Mrs Trigg looked up, her face shocked. "How dreadful," she said. "How could anyone be so cruel?"

"People do that kind of thing all the time," James said sadly. "But at least Holly was saved."

"Holly . . ." Mrs Trigg repeated the name. "That's the name of my cottage."

Mandy nodded. "It was Sandy who found her. She had just been left to die in the snow. She was hurt and really cold when we brought her in. If it hadn't been for Sandy, Holly wouldn't be alive now."

Mrs Trigg looked thoughtful. "It seems that Sandy is quite a clever dog," she remarked.

Mandy nodded. "Oh, he is," she agreed. "And Holly is the sweetest little thing. She has a lovely nature. But she'll have to go to the RSPCA soon."

"And what will happen to her then?"

asked Mrs Trigg, rubbing Holly's ears gently with a finger. Holly snuffled and sneezed. Mrs Trigg laughed.

"They'll try to find a home for her," Mandy explained. "But it's a difficult time of year. Lots of people get puppies at Christmas and then get rid of them when they find out how much work is involved. There are so many abandoned puppies after Christmas that she might not find a home at all."

"And what would happen then?" asked Mrs Trigg.

Mandy laid a hand on Holly's furry head and stroked the puppy's nose. "She would have to be put down," she explained.

Mrs Trigg frowned. "That would be a pity," she said. "Especially after you saved her. She isn't a very young puppy, is she?"

Mandy shook her head. "Holly is about five months old. She's had all her injections and everything – and she's toilet-trained."

Holly nibbled at Mrs Trigg's gloved fingers. "I've never thought pets were very useful," she said thoughtfully.

Mandy rubbed Holly's ears. "They *can* be," she said. "Just think about all the seeing and hearing dogs there are. But the great thing about pets is that they love you and they're good company."

Mrs Trigg looked even more thoughtful. "That's what Amelia Ponsonby said. Holly seems well enough behaved."

"Holly is *gorgeous*," Mandy declared, burying her face in the puppy's soft coat.

"Hmmph!" said Mrs Trigg, suddenly brisk. "Well, I can't stand here all day holding a puppy. It's time Max and I went home."

"And Sandy," added Max.

Mrs Trigg smiled and handed Holly back to Mandy. "And Sandy," she agreed. Mandy and James watched as Mrs Trigg bundled Max out of the unit.

"Do you think there's any chance of us finding a home for Holly before she has to go to the RSPCA?" James asked.

Mandy looked thoughtful. She was still thinking of the way Mrs Trigg had held Holly – and she hadn't even bothered to brush down her coat before she left. "You know, James," she said, "I think we might."

On the day before Christmas Eve Mandy got a surprise telephone call from Mrs Trigg. "Can you and James come round to see me?" the old lady asked.

"But Max is here at Animal Ark," Mandy said. "He and Sandy are saying goodbye to Holly. She has to go to the RSPCA today," she said sadly.

"I know Max is there," Mrs Trigg replied. "And I don't want you to tell him you're coming to see me."

"OK," said Mandy, puzzled. "I'll try to get James alone. He's here, too. We'll both come."

"Make it soon," said Mrs Trigg mysteriously. "I've got a surprise for Max."

Mandy managed to get James alone and told him about the phone call. "But what are we going to say to Max?" James asked.

Mandy thought for a moment. "What if I ask him to do me a special favour and groom Holly before she goes away?"

"That would work," said James. "Holly certainly loves being groomed. She won't let you stop once you've started."

Mandy grinned and went to find Max. As expected, he was more than willing. He didn't even ask her where she was going.

Mandy and James rushed round to Holly Cottage. Mrs Trigg was waiting for them and she opened the door at once. James looked at Blackie.

"Shall I tie him up outside?" he asked.

Mrs Trigg shook her head. "Bring him in. Just don't let him jump on the furniture."

James looked at Mandy as they followed Mrs Trigg into the cottage. Mandy shrugged, then she sniffed. She could smell mince-pies baking – and the scent of pine needles. There was something very odd going on at Holly Cottage.

Mrs Trigg ushered them into the living-room and Mandy gasped. There, in the corner of the room, was the prettiest little Christmas tree Mandy had ever seen. It sat in its own plant pot and its needles were glossy and green. Beside it was a box of

fairy lights and tree decorations.

"A Christmas tree!" James exclaimed.

"Do you think Max will like it?" Mrs Trigg asked anxiously. "It isn't very big."

"It's perfect," James assured her.

"Is that the surprise?" Mandy asked. "Max will love it."

"There's another surprise," Mrs Trigg said, her eyes shining. "It's wonderful news. I got a call from Max's dad this morning. He and Max's mum are going to be here for Christmas after all! Max's mum is coming out of hospital and his dad has unexpectedly been given leave from his work. They're arriving later today."

"Oh, that's wonderful," James exclaimed. "Max will be so happy."

"But don't tell him," Mrs Trigg warned. "I thought I would have a little surprise party this afternoon to celebrate. It's a long time since I had a Christmas party and *years* since I had a tree. I had forgotten how wonderful a real tree smells."

Mandy smiled with delight, then her face fell.

"What is it, Mandy?" Mrs Trigg asked.

"Well," Mandy explained, "it's just that we're all going carol singing this afternoon. Max was going to come, too."

Mrs Trigg pursed her lips. "Well, that's fine," she said at last. "Why don't you all go carol singing and finish up here? Then we can have a party for all the carol singers – and for Max's mum and dad."

"And keep it as a surprise?" asked James.

Mrs Trigg nodded. "When I saw Animal Ark, I realised how much I'd been missing over these last few years in not making much effort over Christmas. Poor Max; my cottage wasn't very Christmassy for him. I want to make up for that, and a party would make it even more like Christmas."

"But Mrs Trigg," Mandy said slowly, "you don't understand. The carol singers are all bringing their pets."

"Pets?" repeated Mrs Trigg.

Mandy nodded. "You know, their dogs and cats – and Amy Fenton's mouse and Jack Gardiner's rabbit."

"There's even a pony," James put in.

Mrs Trigg frowned and Mandy's heart sank. There was no way she would want all those animals in her cottage.

"Well," said Mrs Trigg at last, "I suppose the pony would have to stay outside."

"You mean you would let all the other animals into your cottage?" Mandy squeaked.

Mrs Trigg looked round her living-room. It was bright and cheerful, and not quite as tidy as usual. There were more Christmas decorations spilling out of a box, which was sitting on a chair, and a pile of presents waiting to be wrapped. "I can always clean it up afterwards," she said. "After all, I like a chance to give the cottage a good clean."

Mandy and James looked at each other and laughed.

"Mrs Trigg," said James, pointing to the box on the chair, "would you like us to help you put those decorations up?"

"That would be wonderful, James," Mrs Trigg replied.

Mandy rolled up her sleeves. "OK, where do you want them?" she asked.

Mrs Trigg spread her arms wide. "*Everywhere*, Mandy!"

9

A home for Holly

Mandy had a lot to think about while she and James helped Mrs Trigg with her decorations. As they left Holly Cottage she grabbed James's arm. "James," she said, "do you think *Mrs Trigg* would take Holly?"

James looked at Mandy in surprise. "Mrs Trigg?" he exclaimed. "I know she really likes Sandy – deep down. But would she really want a puppy of her own?"

"She's changed such a lot," Mandy said thoughtfully. "I can't help thinking of the way she looked at Holly. I'm sure she liked her."

James shoved his glasses up on his nose. "Well, we haven't got much time if we're going to try," he said. "Holly will be leaving Animal Ark pretty soon."

"So, let's go," Mandy said. "We've got to ask Mum and Dad."

"I hope we'll get there in time," Mandy gasped as they rushed up the path and into the surgery. They almost collided with Mandy's gran, who was just coming out of the door.

"What's all the hurry?" Gran asked.

"Gran, has Dad left with Holly yet?" Mandy gasped.

"He's just fetching her now. You'll be in time to say a last goodbye."

"Maybe we won't have to," Mandy said hurriedly. "Oh, Gran, Mrs Trigg is going to have a surprise party for Max. His mum and dad are coming home today and she wants the carol singers to go to Holly Cottage after we finish. She's decorating the cottage and baking and – everything."

"Well, well," said Gran. "I'm glad to hear that. I met her yesterday and she was looking a lot more like her old self." Then Gran paused. "Do you think she could do with a bit of help to get ready for the party?"

"I'm sure she could," Mandy said, smiling. "Gran, you're great!"

"You're not so bad yourself," Gran called after Mandy as she rushed into Animal Ark. "I'll get round there right away."

Mr Hope was lifting Holly out of her cage. Emily Hope was with him and so was Max.

"Dad," Mandy gasped, "can we keep Holly just a little while longer?"

Adam Hope frowned. "But we agreed that she should go to the RSPCA today."

"Maybe we won't have to send her at all," James burst out.

Emily Hope smiled. "Now, slow down," she said. "What's all this about?"

"I think I've found a home for Holly," Mandy explained. "I'm almost sure that Mrs Trigg would take her."

"Gran?" Max cried.

Mandy nodded. "She's so much nicer to Sandy now, Max. You know that. And she really liked Holly when she met her – I know she did."

Mrs Hope looked thoughtful. "You said *almost* sure, Mandy," she said. "Haven't you asked her? It's a big risk to take. You know that after Christmas there will be lots more puppies for the RSPCA to find homes for. At least if she goes today there'll be a small chance that somebody might choose her as a pet before Christmas."

Mandy nodded. "I know that, Mum," she said. "But it isn't a very big chance, and I just think that if Mrs Trigg sees Holly again she'll change her mind about having a pet. And it would mean that Holly could stay in Welford. Please – can I try? Please?"

Mr and Mrs Hope looked at each other. Mandy gazed at the little puppy in her father's arms. She couldn't bear to lose Holly entirely.

"I suppose it's worth a try," Mr Hope said at last. "But you mustn't force Mrs Trigg to take her, Mandy."

"Oh, we wouldn't do that," said James.

Max grinned. "They *couldn't* force Gran," he said. "If she says yes, it's because she really wants Holly."

Mandy laid a hand on Holly's silky coat. Max had groomed the little terrier-cross until she gleamed. "Of course she wants Holly," she declared. "She just doesn't *know* it yet!"

Mrs Hope smiled. "All right then,

Mandy," she said. "But if Mrs Trigg *doesn't* want Holly then she'll have to go tomorrow morning. We can't keep her."

Mandy nodded, her face serious again. "I know that, Mum," she said. "But I'm sure I'm right. I'm just sure of it."

Mandy looked at Max. Now all she had to do was keep him at Animal Ark for the afternoon, so that the party would be a surprise. "Let's do some carol practice," she suggested, nudging James. "Then we can all go out singing from here."

"Good idea," said James, taking the hint. "Come on, Max. Let's get the carol sheets."

Mandy looked at James gratefully as he dragged Max out of the door. "I've got another surprise," she announced to her mum and dad, and launched into explanations about the party.

"*Good King Wenceslas looked out*
    On the feast of Stephen . . ."
The carol rang round the village as Mandy and her friends sang as they walked up the snowy main street. Even the animals were

joining in. Duchess miaowed along with the music and Blackie gave a bark. Paddy had tinsel threaded through his bridle and a warm red rug on his back. He whinnied softly. All over the village, people came to their doors to hear the carols.

Mandy was carrying Holly in her arms. Her leg was no longer bandaged, but Mandy wanted to be quite sure the little animal came to no harm. The puppy looked up as a flake of snow settled on her nose. More flakes fell, shining in the light of the lamps the children carried. They only had one more house to go now and, as they approached Holly Cottage, Mandy cuddled Holly closer to her. "Not long now, Holly. You'll soon have a new home, I promise you," she whispered to the puppy.

James opened the gate of Holly Cottage and Jill Redfern started a new carol: "*Ding dong merrily on high . . .*"

They all joined in, the sound floating through the frosty air towards the front door. It opened, flooding the path with light. Mrs Trigg stood there waiting for them.

The children grouped themselves round the door and finished the carol. Max was flushed with pleasure.

Mrs Trigg beamed at them. "That was lovely," she said. "Thank you! Now, come in out of the cold. I've got a surprise for you all."

The children trooped into the house. "Take your shoes off," Mrs Trigg ordered, but she said it with a smile.

Paul tied Paddy to the front porch, making sure the pony was protected from the snow.

Leaving their boots and coats in the hall, the carol singers followed Mrs Trigg through to the living-room. Mandy gasped. The tree twinkled in the corner, the room was festooned with decorations and a fire burned brightly in the hearth. But it wasn't the decorations that made her gasp – it was the table, laden with goodies. Along with plates full of delicious-looking tiny sandwiches and rolls, there were others heaped with mince-pies, gingerbread and little iced cupcakes. A beautifully decorated Christmas cake sat in the middle.

"Gran!" breathed Max.

"I thought you would like a party for your friends," Mrs Trigg told him. "Mandy and James helped me keep it a surprise for you. And Mandy's gran helped with the baking. She even brought round a spare Christmas cake she'd baked, as I didn't have time to bake one. We had great fun decorating it this afternoon!"

"But what about all the *animals*?" Max asked.

Mrs Trigg looked round the little choir. Timmy, Peter Foster's Cairn terrier, bounded up to the table and looked longingly at the goodies. Jack Gardiner's rabbit, Hoppy, poked his head round Jack's arm and waggled his ears, and Amy Fenton's mouse, Minnie, twitched her whiskers.

"Don't worry," said Amy. "I won't let her go. She doesn't like Duchess much." The furry Persian cat stalked over to the table and miaowed.

Mrs Trigg laughed. "Just keep them off the furniture," she said. "There are lots of nice things for the pets, too – in the kitchen."

"What about Paddy?" asked Paul.

"There are carrots and apples," Mrs Trigg told him. "Paddy can share them with Jack's rabbit."

Max was looking as if he couldn't believe his ears. Just then the doorbell rang. Mandy's mum and dad trooped in with Gran and Grandad.

"Now the party can really start," said Mrs Trigg happily. "Come on then – tuck in!"

They didn't need to be told twice. Gran beamed at Mrs Trigg. "I was just saying to Tom that we'll have to get you back on the committee of the Women's Institute, Maggie," she said. "We could do with a good cook like you to help with all our functions."

Mrs Trigg flushed. "Oh, Dorothy, I would really like that," she said, her face lighting up.

Mandy was halfway through a plate of egg sandwiches and mince-pies when Mrs Trigg came over to her. Holly was sitting quietly at Mandy's feet. Mandy bent and fed her a bit of sandwich, then picked the little dog up with one hand, balancing her plate in the other.

"This is the puppy that was abandoned, isn't it?" Mrs Trigg asked.

Mandy nodded innocently. "You'd better say goodbye to her, Mrs Trigg," she said. "I was hoping somebody in Welford would adopt her. She's so sweet. I'll really miss her when she goes. It's such a pity she can't stay here among her friends."

"You'd think *somebody* would want her," Mrs Trigg said. "Just look at her beautiful coat."

"She loves being groomed," Mandy continued, watching Mrs Trigg run her hand through Holly's silky hair.

"She's a lovely little thing," Mrs Trigg said. "I hope she finds a good home." Mandy sighed and deliberately tipped her plate just a little. "Can you take her for a moment, Mrs Trigg?" she asked. "I don't want to spill anything."

Mrs Trigg put out her arms and gathered the little puppy into them. "I'm not very good with animals," she said.

116

Mandy looked at the old lady cradling the puppy. Holly put her head in the crook of Mrs Trigg's arm and yawned. "Oh, I think you are," Mandy said softly. "Holly likes you."

Mrs Trigg looked down at the puppy wonderingly. "Do you really think so?" she asked.

The doorbell rang again. Mrs Trigg went to answer it. A man and woman came into the room, shaking the snow from their coats.

"Oops, sorry about the mess, Mum," the man said, hugging Mrs Trigg. "We were in a rush to see Max."

"Come in! Come in!" Mrs Trigg welcomed them, her eyes sparkling with happiness. "Max, here's another surprise for you."

"Dad! *Mum!*" Max yelled, flying across the room. "How did you get here, Dad? Are you better now, Mum?"

Max's mum held out her arms and Max hugged her while she explained how she got out of hospital early.

"And I got all my work finished early too,

Max," his father explained, ruffling his son's hair. "Mum and I wanted so much to be with you for Christmas."

Max turned, his arms round both his parents. "What a Christmas present!" he said.

His mum looked around. "Oh, you're having a party," she said, looking surprised.

Max's dad grinned. "Look at all these animals, Mum," he said. "This is great. Max won't want to come home with us after Christmas if he's been having such a good time here!"

Max looked at his gran. "Gran has been great," he said. "She's been really kind to Sandy."

Mrs Trigg blushed. "Oh, I don't know about that, Max," she said. "I wasn't very good with him at first."

"That doesn't matter now," Max said. "Sandy thinks you're great."

Sandy scampered across the room and tried to undo Mrs Trigg's shoe laces. "Down, Sandy," Mrs Trigg said, but she was smiling. "That's his favourite game!" she said.

Sandy sat down and looked up at her, wagging his tail.

"And you've got a dog of your own," Max's mum said, coming over to stand beside her mother-in-law and stroke the puppy in her arms.

"Oh, no . . ." Mrs Trigg began.

"Good for you, Mum," her son said. "I've thought for a long while that you should get a pet to keep you company, and a dog is perfect. What's its name?"

"Holly," said Mrs Trigg, looking confused.

"Just like the cottage," Max's mum said, smiling. She had soft brown hair and blue eyes – like Max.

"But she isn't mine," said Mrs Trigg.

Mandy looked up at her. "She *could* be, though," she said gently.

Mrs Trigg looked down at the puppy in her arms. Holly opened her eyes and gazed adoringly back, then she licked Mrs Trigg's hand.

Mandy waited, holding her breath.

"Do you think she would *like* to stay at

Holly Cottage with me?" Mrs Trigg asked.

"I'm sure she would," Mandy replied. "You'd be rescuing her, Mrs Trigg."

"And she would be such good company," Mrs Trigg answered. "I think I'm going to miss Sandy when he goes."

"I'll bring Sandy to see Holly lots of times," Max promised. "They're good friends."

Mrs Trigg looked around at all the eager faces. "I'd love to have her! What an unexpected Christmas gift!" she said.

"And you've given Holly the best Christmas present as well," Mandy assured her. "A home!" She looked across at her mum and dad; they were both smiling. Adam Hope gave her the thumbs-up sign.

"You've given *me* the best Christmas ever, Gran," said Max. "I've never had such a good party."

Mandy and James looked at each other. "A pets' party," Mandy declared. "The best party possible!"

Kitten Kisses

Kitten Kisses

Special thanks to Narinder Dhami

Text copyright © 1998 Working Partners Ltd
Created by Working Partners Ltd, London W6 0QT
Original series created by Ben M. Baglio
Illustrations copyright © 1998 Paul Howard

First published as a single volume in Great Britain in 2002
by Hodder Children's Books

1

A very friendly kitten

"I *love* Christmas!" Mandy Hope said happily. She pulled a long, shimmering strand of silver tinsel from the box of decorations. "Look, James, there's loads of this. It's going to look great on the tree."

James Hunter, Mandy's best friend, nodded. He pushed his glasses more firmly up his nose and bent over the box of decorations. "I'm glad I left Blackie at home," he remarked. "He'd have tried to run off with everything!" Blackie was James's naughty Labrador puppy.

Mandy started to hang the tinsel on the tree, while James burrowed deeper into the box. "What's this, Mandy?" he asked, holding up a large plastic container.

Mandy looked down at him and grinned. "Open it and see," she told him.

James prised the lid off the container and peered inside. Then he burst out laughing. "Wooden animals to hang on the tree!" he exclaimed, tipping them carefully out on to the floor. There were dogs, cats, rabbits and even reindeer, all beautifully painted and sparkling with glitter. "They're brilliant, Mandy."

Mandy glanced round the surgery waiting-room. "Well, this *is* Animal Ark!" she pointed out. She thought that Animal Ark was the best place to live in the whole world. Her mum and dad were both vets, and the surgery where they worked was built on to the back of their cottage in the village of

Welford. Mandy was mad about animals, and she couldn't imagine living anywhere else. With Christmas not far off, her parents had said that she and James could decorate the Christmas tree in the waiting-room. As Saturday morning surgery was nearly over, they'd already made a start.

"Has my last appointment arrived yet?" asked Adam Hope, popping his head round the door of his consulting-room.

"Not yet, Dad." Mandy hung the last wooden animal on the tree and stood back to admire it. "What do you think?"

"Very nice indeed," said Mr Hope. "And the wooden animals look great, just right for Animal Ark." He smiled at Mandy and James. "Let me know if anyone turns up with a reindeer, will you?"

Mandy and James laughed as Mr Hope disappeared back into his room.

"Look, James! It's snowing again." Mandy pointed excitedly at the window. The village was already covered with a thick blanket of snow, and now even more large, white flakes were falling silently from the grey sky.

"I can't wait for Christmas," James sighed, as Mandy searched through the box of decorations again. "There's *still* a week to go. That's ages."

"But there's lots of exciting things happening before Christmas," Mandy reminded him, pulling out a large silver star. "Don't forget, there's the Christmas party at school next Thursday."

"Oh, yes," James said happily. "*And* we've got that special surprise at the party. Everyone at school's talking about it."

"What do you think it can be?" Mandy asked. She fetched a chair, and stood on it to fix the star carefully to the top of the tree.

James shrugged. "I don't know," he replied. "But—"

"I know," Mandy broke in teasingly. "You can't *wait!*"

Suddenly the front door opened and a flurry of snow swept into the warm waiting-room. A dark-haired girl in a red coat hurried in, followed by a tall man carrying a cat basket. Snow dusted their outdoor clothes like icing sugar, showing that they had walked through the village to the surgery.

James nudged Mandy as the girl and her father went over to the receptionist's desk, unwinding their scarves and pulling off their gloves. "That's Tina Cunningham and her dad," he whispered.

Mandy nodded. Tina was in James's class at school, and she had riding lessons at the local stables where Mandy went to Pony Club. But she was quite shy, so neither Mandy nor James knew her very well.

"We'd better fetch Jean," Mandy said to James. Jean Knox, the Animal Ark receptionist, had popped into the store cupboard to do some stock checking before the Christmas holiday.

"I'll go," James offered, and he hurried across the waiting-room.

Mandy hurried over to the Cunninghams and smiled at Tina, who returned the smile shyly. "Hello there," she said. "Jean won't be long."

"Sorry we're late," Mr Cunningham apologised. "Peaches hid behind the sofa and we couldn't get her out!"

"Peaches? What a lovely name," Mandy said, peering eagerly into the cat basket. An adorable kitten stared back at her with big, unblinking green eyes. Her thick coat was a beautiful ginger colour marked with darker marmalade stripes.

"Oh, isn't she gorgeous?" Mandy gasped, turning to Tina.

Tina nodded proudly, as Peaches sat up tall and began to wash herself with busy licks. "She's two months old today," she explained. "When she was born, she was the smallest of the litter, and she wasn't very well. She's a lot better now, but we've brought her for a check-up."

Mandy smiled. Tina seemed much less shy when she was talking about Peaches. She obviously loved the little kitten to bits. "Would she mind if I stroked her?" Mandy asked.

Tina and her dad looked at each other and laughed. Mandy wondered why. "Of course you can," said Tina.

Mandy pushed her fingers carefully through the wire front of the basket. Peaches immediately started to purr loudly. She rubbed her fluffy head against Mandy's hand and began licking her fingers. Mandy smiled at the feel of the kitten's rough little tongue on her skin. "I *did* have a bath this morning, Peaches," she laughed. "I don't need a wash, thank you!"

"Oh, Peaches licks *everything*," grinned

Tina, just as Jean Knox and James came back from the store cupboard.

"Good morning," said Jean, picking up her glasses from the desk. "It's the Cunninghams, isn't it?"

"With Peaches," Mandy added. "James, isn't she cute?"

James nodded and pushed his fingers into the basket, just as Mandy had done. Purring like an engine, the kitten pounced on James's fingers and grabbed one of them between her soft little pads. Then she licked it busily.

Mandy and Tina laughed at the surprised look on James's face. "Peaches likes licking things," Mandy explained.

"We think it's because her mum licked her so much when she was born," Mr Cunningham explained. "Peaches was so weak that her mum gave her lots of extra attention, and that included lots of grooming."

"Dad said it was just like a mummy kissing their baby!" said Tina. "I think that's why Peaches got better, because her mum licked her so much."

The door of the consulting-room opened, and Mandy's dad came out. "Hello again," he said to the Cunninghams, taking the notes Jean handed him. "Would you like to come through, and we'll see how Peaches is getting on?"

"There's nothing really wrong with her, is there, Dad?" Mandy asked anxiously.

Mr Hope shook his head. "No, but we've had to keep an eye on her because she was the runt of the litter. She was quite underweight at first, but she seems to be eating well now, and getting bigger."

Tina glanced at Mandy and James. "Would you like to . . ." she began hesitantly. Turning pink, she stopped and whispered something to her dad. Mr Cunningham nodded and smiled.

"Would you like to come in with us?" Tina finished in a rush, looking at Mandy and James.

"If Mr Hope doesn't mind, of course," added Mr Cunningham.

Mandy's face lit up. "Can we, Dad?" she asked.

Mr Hope nodded. "Of course," he said, pushing open the door of his consulting-room. "The more, the merrier!"

Mandy beamed as she followed Tina and Mr Cunningham inside. She'd fallen in love with the kitten already, and she couldn't wait to hear how Peaches was getting on. Although, looking at the kitten's friendly little face, there didn't seem to be *too* much wrong with her!

2

A Christmas mystery

"Right, let's have a look at you, Peaches."
Mr Hope lifted the cat basket on to the
examining-table and began to unlatch it.
Peaches jumped to her paws and waited,
trying to lick Mr Hope's fingers as he
undid the catches.

Mandy watched as her dad swung open
the door of the basket. Peaches padded

out eagerly and looked round the room, her almond-shaped green eyes wide with interest. Then she bent her head, sniffed the table and gave it a couple of licks. Mandy and James burst out laughing.

"Peaches did that last time we came here," said Tina.

Mr Hope scooped up the kitten and held her in his hands for a moment. "She's definitely putting on weight," he said. "I can tell that she's heavier even without putting her on the scales. That's a very good sign."

"My friend's got a kitten the same age as Peaches," said Tina. "And her kitten's a bit bigger."

"Yes, Peaches still has some catching up to do," Mr Hope agreed. "But she's doing very well, Tina, so don't worry."

Mandy's dad weighed the kitten, and then carefully examined her eyes and ears. Peaches kept grabbing Mr Hope's fingers with her front paws and trying to wash them.

"Do you *ever* stop licking things, Peaches?" Mandy laughed.

"No, she doesn't!" said Mr Cunningham. "And we're a bit worried about it." He glanced at Mr Hope. "She licks everything around the house," he went on, "and she spends hours grooming herself too."

Mr Hope put Peaches down on the table, and the kitten immediately began to wash herself thoroughly, as if she'd heard every word that they'd said.

"Does it matter if she licks herself so much?" asked Tina. "It won't make her tongue sore, will it?"

"Oh, no," said Mr Hope. "But when cats swallow lots of hairs, a furball forms in their tummy. It makes them very sick."

"Oh dear." Tina looked worried.

"But Peaches' coat is quite short," Mr Hope went on. "And if you brush her regularly, it shouldn't be too much of a problem, however much she washes herself."

"I brush her nearly every day, don't I, Dad?" said Tina proudly.

"I bet Peaches tries to lick the brush, though, doesn't she?" Mandy joked, and Tina laughed.

"Yes, she does," she agreed.

Mr Hope put the kitten gently back into the basket. "Peaches might grow out of the habit of licking everything when she gets a bit older," he said with a smile. "But it won't hurt her too much. As long as you keep her away from things which aren't any good for her!"

"Did you hear that, Tina?" said Mr Cunningham, as he lifted the cat basket off the table. "You'd better be careful this afternoon when you and your mum make those Christmas decorations. I don't think glue and glitter will be very good for Peaches' tummy!"

Mandy and James both looked interested.

"What are the decorations for?" asked James. "Are they for your Christmas tree?"

Tina shook her head. "No, they're for the Christmas party at school," she explained. "My mum's helping to decorate the hall, because she's in the PTA."

Mandy remembered that the mums and dads who belonged to the Parent Teacher Association helped with the party every year.

"What are you going to make?" she asked.

"Oh, some paper chains and glittery stars and lots of other stuff," Tina replied. She smiled a little timidly at Mandy and James. "If you aren't doing anything else, maybe you'd like to come and help?"

"That's a good idea," said Tina's father. "The more people who are around to stop Peaches licking the Christmas decorations, the better!"

Mandy and James looked at each other in delight. "We'd love to come and help," Mandy said eagerly. "Is that all right, Dad?"

"Fine with me," replied Mr Hope, as he wiped down the table with disinfectant. "I'll let your mum know where you are." Mrs Hope had gone Christmas shopping in Walton, the nearest town to Welford. "One of us will pop round and pick you up later on."

Mandy turned to James. "Come on, let's get our coats," she said.

Mandy and James hurried into the Hopes' cottage through the connecting door and grabbed their coats, scarves and gloves. With all this snow, they needed to wrap up warmly. Then they pulled on their wellies and dashed back into the surgery, where Tina and her dad were waiting with Peaches.

"Brr!" Mandy shivered as Mr Cunningham opened the door. "It's even colder than yesterday."

The snow had almost stopped falling, and now there were only a few stray flakes drifting down here and there. It was so cold that Mandy could see her breath like a cloud in the icy air. But even though it was freezing cold, the village looked very beautiful and Christmassy with the snow glistening on the trees and the rooftops. The fields around the village were covered with a heavy layer of snow too, as if someone had hidden them under a thick, white quilt. Mandy hoped that the snow would last until Christmas Day. It didn't really *feel* like Christmas unless there was snow.

"Are you going to buy Peaches a Christmas present?" Mandy asked Tina as they walked though Welford, the fresh snow crunching under their feet.

Tina nodded. "I've been saving my pocket-money," she said. "Mum's going to take me to the pet shop in Walton to buy it."

"What are you going to get her?" James asked curiously.

"Something she can lick!" Tina smiled.

"Good idea," said Mandy, peeping into the cat basket. Tina had wrapped Peaches up snugly in her cosy blanket, and the kitten

seemed quite happy to stay there, with just her little ginger head poking out.

"Is your mum coming to the party on Thursday?" Mandy asked Tina, as they crossed the village green.

"Yes, she is," replied Tina. "She's going to put up the decorations just before, and then stay to watch the— the party," she finished.

"Oh!" James said suddenly, as if an idea had just struck him. "Tina, have you heard about the special surprise that everyone's talking about? You know, the one that's going to happen at the party?"

Mandy glanced at Tina, and was puzzled to see she had turned bright red.

"Yes, I've heard about it," mumbled Tina, her head down.

"Well, I was wondering if your mum knew what the surprise was." James stared eagerly at Tina. "I mean, she's in the PTA so maybe she knows what's going on. The teachers won't tell us *anything*."

Tina looked even more embarrassed and didn't say anything.

"I think it's better to wait until the party, don't you, James?" Mr Cunningham said quickly. "After all, it's meant to be a surprise. And it won't be if you find out beforehand!"

"Oh, OK," sighed James. "I suppose you're right."

Mandy stole a sideways glance at Tina and her dad as they walked on through the snow. James hadn't noticed anything, but it seemed to Mandy that maybe Tina and her dad had a very good idea what the big surprise was going to be! Mandy smiled to herself. It was quite a Christmas mystery . . .

3

Lost in the snow

The Cunninghams' house was in Willow Lane, not far from Lilac Cottage where Mandy's gran and grandad lived. By the time they reached the house, Mandy's nose felt like an icicle. Even her hands in their fleecy blue gloves were numb. Mandy peeked into the cat basket again, but Peaches was still wrapped up in her blanket, and looked as warm as toast.

"Let's all go inside and have a nice hot drink," said Mr Cunningham, fumbling in his pocket for his keys. But suddenly the door opened and a tall, fair-haired woman stood on the doorstep.

"Come in," she said. "You must be freezing."

"Mum, this is Mandy and James," Tina told her, as everyone trooped into the hall. "They've come to help make the Christmas decorations."

"Oh, good," said Mrs Cunningham cheerfully. "That's very kind of you both."

Mandy unwound her scarf from round her neck. The house was warm and welcoming after the frosty air outside. She could see a log fire burning in the living-room, and a large Christmas tree stood next to the sofa, its fairy lights twinkling in lots of different colours.

"How's Peaches?" asked Tina's mum.

"She's fine," said Tina. "She's put on some more weight."

"I'll take her into the kitchen and give her

something to eat," said Mrs Cunningham, unlatching the basket and lifting out Peaches. "You go and get warm by the fire, and I'll bring you some hot chocolate."

"Oh, yum!" said James. Then he blushed when everyone smiled.

"And I've got some banana cake too," Tina's mum added, as she carried the kitten off towards the kitchen. "Now, Peaches, don't lick my hair. I've told you about that before!"

"Come on in," said Tina, leading Mandy and James into the living-room as Mr Cunningham disappeared upstairs. There was a large table at one end of the room, covered with sheets of coloured foil and card, tubes of glitter, paints, scissors and glue.

"It looks like Mum's got everything ready," said Tina excitedly.

"What shall we make first?" Mandy asked, sitting down on one of the chairs.

"Well, paper chains are quite easy," replied Tina.

"I can do that," offered James. "We made them at school last year."

"Shall we make some stars, Tina?" Mandy suggested. "If we cut them out of card, then we could cover them with glitter."

"Good idea," Tina agreed.

James collected some sheets of foil and started cutting them into strips. Meanwhile, Mandy and Tina each took a pencil and tried to draw some stars on a piece of card. But it was much more difficult than it looked.

"This is awful!" Mandy sighed, staring at the third wobbly star she'd just drawn. "I can't get it right, even with a ruler."

"It's really hard to get the star the same size all round," complained Tina. "Look, mine's got three tiny points and three big ones!"

Just then Tina's mum came in with a tray, bearing three steaming mugs of hot chocolate, as well as a large rectangular cake sliced into chunks. "Oh, you've started already," she said with a smile, putting the tray down on the table. "Goodness me, James, that looks marvellous."

James grinned and held up his paper chain. He was using three colours, red, green and

silver, and he'd already made quite a long chain by looping the foil strips and gluing them together.

"We're not doing very well, Mum," said Tina gloomily, pointing at the piece of card she was drawing on.

"Our stars don't look a bit like stars," Mandy added.

"Well, maybe I can help," said Tina's mum, picking up a pencil. Mandy and Tina drank their hot chocolate and watched closely as Mrs Cunningham drew a large triangle on a thick piece of card and cut it out.

"But that doesn't look anything like a star!" protested Tina. Mandy was secretly thinking the same thing.

"This is just a template to draw round," Mrs Cunningham replied. "Now comes the magic part." She put the triangle on top of another piece of card and drew round it. "That makes three points of the star," she explained. Then she turned the triangle upside-down, and placed it on top of the first one so that it made the other three points of the star. "And there you are," Tina's mum went on, lifting the template off the card. "Not a bad-looking star, even if I say so myself!"

"That's great, Mrs Cunningham," Mandy said admiringly. "We can make loads of stars now!"

Mrs Cunningham made another triangle template, and Mandy and Tina set to work again. Mandy was just proudly completing her very first star when she felt something licking the leg of her jeans. She jumped, and dropped the tube of glitter she was holding.

"Oh!" she gasped, bending down to look under the table. Peaches was sitting there, looking very pleased with herself. She stared up at Mandy with a loud *miaow*.

"Peaches, what are you doing here?" scolded Tina, leaning down to scoop up the kitten. "I thought you were in the kitchen."

"Don't let Peaches anywhere near the decorations," warned Mrs Cunningham, as the kitten tried to wriggle her way out of Tina's arms. The shiny foil that James was using had caught Peaches' attention, and she was staring at it as it shimmered in the light.

"I'd better take her back to the kitchen." Tina stood up, but suddenly Peaches struggled free and leaped out of Tina's arms on to the table. She landed right on top of the glittery star that Mandy had just made, getting a few bits of loose glitter on her paws.

"Don't let her lick it!" Mandy cried in alarm. She made a grab for Peaches, and managed to get hold of her before she had a chance to lick anything. But by this time she had bright silver glitter on her ears too, and on the tip of her tail.

"She looks like a fairy kitten!" Mandy laughed.

"I'll take her into the kitchen and get her cleaned up," said Mrs Cunningham, taking charge of Peaches. "Call me if you need any help."

For the next hour, Mandy, James and Tina worked very hard on the decorations. James made three long paper chains, and Mandy and Tina drew a whole row of glittering stars. They also made some jolly Father Christmasses, painting them red and using fluffy white cotton wool for Santa's beard.

"I think that's quite enough for today," said Mrs Cunningham, coming back into the living-room and surveying the busy table. "Well done, all of you. Bring the decorations into the kitchen, and we'll dry them off. I've made some sandwiches for lunch."

Mandy, James and Tina carefully collected up everything they'd made and carried them into the kitchen. Peaches was curled up cosily in her basket by the Aga, but she lifted her head and mewed with delight when she saw them. Mrs Cunningham began to lay the decorations on top of the stove. The stove lids were down, covering the hotplates, so that the decorations wouldn't get too hot. Meanwhile Mandy, James and Tina sat at the kitchen table to have their lunch.

"What shall we do now?" asked Tina, when they'd finished all the sandwiches.

"We could go outside and build a snowman," James suggested.

"Good idea!" said Mandy and Tina together.

Mandy looked out of the back door as she pulled on her wellies. The snow had stopped falling, but it looked quite deep. They'd be able to make a brilliant snowman.

"Will Peaches come outside with us?" she asked.

Tina shook her head. "No, she hates the snow," she replied, unlocking the back door. "She'll probably watch us through the door."

They went outside and closed the door behind them. Mandy laughed when, a

154

moment later, she saw Peaches bound out of her basket and rush over to peer through the glass panel at the bottom of the door.

"Look, she's licking the glass!" Mandy pointed out with a grin.

James was already rolling a snowball around the lawn, making it bigger and bigger. "Come on, you two," he called.

They set to work. It didn't take the three of them long to roll a big, round ball of snow for the snowman's body, and then a smaller one for his head.

"We need some pebbles to make his nose and eyes," Mandy said. While James and Tina lifted the snowman's head on to his body, she went off to find some pebbles. Most of the garden was covered with snow, but she spotted a gravel path at the side of the house. Because it was quite sheltered, the snow wasn't as deep here, and the gravel was showing through.

Mandy walked over to the side of the house, leaving a trail of footprints in the clean, white snow. There was a large woodpile on the other side of the path, the logs neatly stacked one on top of the other. Tina's dad must have been very busy cutting wood for their fire, Mandy thought as she bent down to pick up some stones.

"*Mee-ow!*"

Mandy smiled when she heard the kitten's voice. Peaches must have ventured outside after all. "Peaches?" she called, expecting to see the little kitten appear round the side of the house. But there was no sign of her.

"*Meeow!*"

Mandy's eyes widened as she heard the kitten calling again. Where was that noise coming from? It sounded as if it was close by.

There was another soft mew. It was coming from the woodpile! Mandy dashed over and peered round the end of it. At once her heart began to beat faster. There, curled up on a grubby piece of cardboard between the woodpile and the fence, were three tiny kittens.

4

The missing mum

"Oh!" Mandy clapped a hand to her mouth in surprise. She stared down at the three kittens, who huddled together, shivering. Mandy could tell that they weren't very old because their eyes weren't fully open yet. One was black, one was white with ginger patches and the third was a beautiful smoky grey with darker stripes.

"Oh, you poor things," Mandy whispered, a lump in her throat. She turned round and shouted down the garden. "Tina! James! Come here, quick!"

"What's the matter?" asked James, hurrying over with Tina close behind.

"Look." Mandy pointed behind the woodpile at the kittens, and James and Tina both gasped.

"Are they all right?" Tina said anxiously.

"Where's their mum?" asked James.

"I don't know, but we need to get them inside and warm them up," Mandy said urgently.

"I'll go and tell Mum," said Tina, and she ran off round the side of the house.

"They look cold," James said in a worried voice.

"Let's wrap them in our scarves," Mandy suggested. She squeezed behind the woodpile and bent down to pick up the black kitten, who was nearest. The kitten mewed loudly as Mandy handed it to James, followed by the ginger and white one.

While James was settling the first two

kittens snugly inside his jacket, Mandy reached for the tiny, smoky grey kitten. She bit her lip as she lifted it up and felt how thin it was. Quickly she wrapped the kitten in her warm blue scarf, just as Tina ran round the side of the house towards them.

"Mum says to bring the kittens straight in," she panted. "And your mum's just come, Mandy."

Mandy felt a rush of relief. Her mum would be able to tell if the kittens needed any treatment.

Mrs Cunningham and Mrs Hope were waiting for them by the back door. "Come inside, quickly," said Mrs Cunningham, opening the door wider. "Are the poor little things all right?"

"I don't know," Mandy gasped, as she and James rushed into the warm kitchen. She looked anxiously at her mum. "Oh, Mum, the kittens are *so* cold, and they're really thin, especially this one." She unwrapped her scarf and a tiny, fluffy grey head came into view. James had already undone his coat and put his two kittens down on the kitchen table.

"It looks like I arrived just in time, doesn't it?" said Emily Hope. "Let me have a look at them. Goodness me, they *are* tiny, aren't they? They can only be about four or five days old."

Everyone stood round the table watching as Mrs Hope checked the kittens over. James's kittens seemed to perk up now that they were in a warm place, and they nosed their way blindly round the table on their stumpy, unsteady legs, mewling loudly. The tiniest kitten sat in a heap, shivering. Mandy thought it looked utterly miserable.

"Well, this one's a girl," said Mrs Hope as she examined the grey kitten. "And the other two are boys. They're in remarkably good shape, considering how cold it is outside."

Mandy's heart thumped with relief.

"But they're a bit underweight, especially this one," Mrs Hope went on. She gently stroked the grey kitten's head. "She's definitely the runt of the litter."

"Just like Peaches when she was born," said Tina.

Just then there was a loud *miaow* at their feet. Mandy looked down to see Peaches standing on her back legs with her front paws against the table leg, trying in vain to see what was going on.

"Peaches wants to make friends with the kittens," laughed Tina.

"I think the kittens have had enough excitement for one day," Mandy's mum said with a smile. "It might be best to keep Peaches away from them for the moment."

"OK," agreed Tina. "I'll shut her in the

living-room." She picked up Peaches and carried her out.

"Mrs Hope, will the mother cat come back for her kittens?" asked James.

Mandy's mum frowned. "That's a good question. It's very unusual for a mother cat to abandon her kittens, but that does seem to have happened here. The kittens certainly don't look like they've been feeding regularly."

"Maybe something's happened to their mum," Mandy suggested, picking up the black kitten who had strayed too close to the edge of the table.

"Yes, that's possible," Mrs Hope agreed. "It's quite likely that the mother might need some medical attention herself." She turned to Mrs Cunningham and to Tina, who had just come back into the room. "Have you noticed any stray cats hanging about your garden?" she asked.

Tina and her mum looked at each other, then shook their heads. "No, I'm afraid not," said Mrs Cunningham.

Mandy couldn't help feeling worried all

over again. The kittens were safe, but what about their mother? She could be lying somewhere, injured or ill. "What's going to happen to the kittens now?" she asked anxiously.

"Well, they're going to need a lot of care and attention," replied her mum. "They'll have to be fed regularly for a start, as their mother isn't here to feed them."

"We could keep them here for the time being," offered Mrs Cunningham.

Tina's face lit up. "Oh, Mum, can we?" she asked, her eyes shining.

"Yes, I think so," said her mum with a smile. "It seems a shame to take them out into that snow again, that's for sure."

"Well, it would be a good solution to the problem," agreed Mandy's mum. "At least then the kittens would be here if their mum does come back."

Mandy looked at James in delight, and he grinned back at her.

"Do we have to bottle-feed them?" asked Tina, and Mrs Hope nodded.

"I can bring you some bottles and some

milk substitute," she said. "We have plenty at the surgery."

"Just tell us exactly what to do," said Mrs Cunningham, going over to her larder. "I've got a cardboard box in here that would make a warm bed," she went on, pulling open the door. "And, Tina, there are some old towels in the bottom of the airing-cupboard. Could you fetch them, please?"

"The kittens look tired," Mandy said, as Tina dashed out of the kitchen. The grey kitten yawned, showing her pink tongue and tiny white teeth. Even the two boys had stopped roaming around and were sitting quietly, leaning against each other.

When Tina came back, Mandy and James helped her to tuck the towels into the cardboard box her mum had found. The box was big, and quite deep so that the kittens couldn't climb out. James and Tina each put one of the boys on to the soft towel, and then Mandy gently popped their little sister down next to them. All three snuggled up cosily together, and in a moment they were all fast asleep.

"We ought to give them names," Mandy said.

"I was thinking about that," said James. "What about Freckle for the one with the patches? He's got a few small spots right next to his nose!"

"I'd like to call the black one Banjo," said Tina. "My gran used to have a black cat called that."

"Mandy, why don't *you* name the other kitten?" James suggested.

Mandy stared into the box. The kitten was so pretty that she deserved a *special* name, but Mandy's mind was a complete blank. She liked the name Jasmine, but it seemed a very big name for such a tiny kitten. She thought she should choose something light and pretty and silvery-grey, just like the kitten's fur.

"I've got it," Mandy said suddenly. "How about Cobweb?"

"Perfect!" said Tina, a big smile on her face.

"That sounds lovely," said Mandy's mum. She stood up and picked up her coat. "Come

on, you two. I'll collect some bottles and milk substitute from the surgery and bring them round in a little while. Those kittens are going to be hungry when they wake up!"

"Come and see the kittens tomorrow," said Tina, as Mandy and James put on their coats.

"We will," Mandy promised.

It was the middle of the afternoon by now, and the sun was beginning to set. It was even colder than it had been in the morning, and Mandy shivered as they walked down the Cunninghams' path.

"We're going to have to walk home," said Mrs Hope. "Your dad needed the Land-rover to visit a farm."

"We don't mind," Mandy said. "We can look out for the kittens' mum while we're walking through the village," she added hopefully.

"That's a good idea," agreed James.

As they walked along the road, Mandy and James kept a sharp look-out for any cats wandering about. But there wasn't a single one to be seen. Mandy was very disappointed.

"I expect they're all indoors," said James, as they reached his house. "I know Benji will be!" Benji was James's cat.

"Yes, but if the kittens' mum is a stray, she won't have a home to go to," Mandy pointed out, biting her lip. She stared across the snow-covered green. Somewhere out there was the kittens' mum. The kittens were being looked after now, but Mandy still felt worried. Was their mother safe and well, or had something happened to her?

5

Pumpkins and puppeteers

"Mandy, we're going over to the Cunninghams now," Mrs Hope called from the kitchen. "You and James had better get your coats and wellies on."

"OK," Mandy called back. She hurried out of the living-room with James behind her. It was the following day, and James had come over for Sunday lunch. Mrs Hope had promised that she would take them over to Tina's house in the afternoon, and they couldn't *wait* to see the kittens again.

Mandy and James dashed into the kitchen to get their wellies, which were standing by the back door.

Adam Hope, who was doing the washing-up, raised his eyebrows at them. "I didn't know you were so keen to help me with washing-up!" he teased.

"Oh, Dad," Mandy laughed. "You know Mum said we didn't have to, this time. We're going to see the kittens."

"I hope they're all doing well," said Mr Hope, as he rinsed a plate. "It's a shame we haven't found the mother yet."

"Maybe she'll turn up today," James said hopefully.

At that moment Mandy's mum came through the connecting door from the surgery. "I've found some more of that milk substitute," she said, holding it up. "I *thought* we had another couple of packets in the stock cupboard." Mandy and her mum had popped back to the Cunninghams the previous afternoon to drop off the bottles and milk. The kittens had still been asleep, so Mandy hadn't seen them feeding yet. She hoped that they were all drinking lots of milk, especially Cobweb. It would help her to get bigger and stronger.

"It's even colder today, isn't it?" said James, as they went outside to the Land-rover. The sun was shining and the sky was blue, but the air was still freezing and their breath hung in frosty clouds.

Mandy nodded. "It's a good thing we found the kittens yesterday," she said, looking solemn. She couldn't bear to think of them out in the cold, all alone without their mother.

When they arrived at the Cunninghams' house, Tina's mum answered the door. "Come in," she said. "I'm afraid we've got quite a lot going on today! I hope you don't mind."

Mandy wondered what she meant. "How are the kittens?" she asked.

"Doing very well," replied Tina's mum. "They're asleep at the moment, but they'll be awake for a feed very soon, I'm sure! Tina's in the living-room with Peaches." Mrs Cunningham smiled broadly, and Mandy wondered why she looked so amused. "Do take off your coats and go right in."

Mandy and James were hanging up their coats, when James nudged her. "Can you hear something?" he said in a low voice.

Mandy listened hard. At first she couldn't hear anything, then, very faintly, she heard the sound of piano music tinkling away behind the living-room door. Suddenly a voice shouted, "*I am your Fairy Godmother, Cinderella!*"

Mandy laughed. "Tina must be watching TV," she said to James, as Mrs Cunningham opened the door to the living-room.

Mandy stared into the room, hardly able to believe her eyes. Tina was sitting on the sofa with Peaches on her lap, but she wasn't watching TV. The room looked completely different to yesterday, when they had been making decorations in there.

The big dining-table had been moved, and

a large puppet theatre, like a Punch and
Judy show but bigger, stood at one end of
the living-room. The theatre was brightly
painted, and it had a wide stage with red
velvet curtains at each side. On the stage
were two puppets, a beautiful, golden-
haired fairy in a shimmering silver dress,
and a girl dressed in rags. At the front of
the stage was a big, round pumpkin.

As Mandy and James watched open-mouthed, the fairy announced, "You *shall* go to the ball, Cinderella!" She tapped the pumpkin with her silver wand. There was a flash of pink smoke and a loud BANG, which made Mandy and James jump. As the smoke drifted away, Mandy realised that the pumpkin had gone. A gleaming golden coach stood in its place!

"Isn't it great?" said Tina, jumping up with Peaches in her arms. She laughed when she saw the looks of amazement on Mandy and James's faces.

"Where did all *this* come from?" gasped James, staring at the puppet theatre.

There were rustling noises from behind the theatre, and suddenly two people popped out, grinning. One was a tall, fair-haired man in his early twenties, who looked a bit like Tina's mum, and the other was a young woman with silver-rimmed glasses and a shock of ginger hair.

"This is my brother Matthew," said Mrs Cunningham. "And his girlfriend, Alex."

"We're puppeteers," explained Matthew.

"In case you hadn't guessed!" his girlfriend added.

"Wow!" James's eyes were shining. "I've never met a puppeteer before."

"Me neither," said Mandy, staring at the puppet theatre with interest. "Are you doing a show in Welford?"

Matthew and Alex laughed and exchanged a glance.

"Mum, please can I tell Mandy and James the secret?" begged Tina. "I'm sure they won't tell anybody else."

"I think we'll have to," replied Mrs Cunningham, her eyes twinkling. "They'll be coming round to see the kittens, so they're bound to find out sooner or later!"

"Find out what?" Mandy and James said together.

"Uncle Matt and Alex are going to do their puppet show at the school Christmas party," Tina burst out. "*That's* the big surprise!"

"Oh!" James looked thrilled. "That'll be great, won't it, Mandy?"

"Brilliant!" Mandy agreed. "Is it the story of Cinderella?"

"That's right — hence the pumpkin!" laughed Matt. "We're staying here for the next few days, so you'll probably see a few more rehearsals. But remember, not a word to anyone! The teachers want to keep it a secret."

"We promise," Mandy grinned.

"I liked the special effects," said James. "How did you make all that smoke?"

"We've got some special smoke bombs," Matt explained. "When we set them off, it gives us just enough time to get the pumpkin off stage, and put the coach in its place."

"You were really quick," said James admiringly.

"We have to be," Alex told him. "It takes two of us to get the coach into position, so we have to take the puppets off our hands, then put them back on again really fast."

"We've got quite a few other tricks up our sleeves too," added Matt, "but you'll have to wait until the Christmas party for those!"

"I might pop over to the party myself,"

Emily Hope said with a smile. "The show looks marvellous."

"It's coming along nicely," replied Alex. "As long as we keep the puppets away from Peaches. She got hold of Cinderella this morning, and nearly licked her to bits!"

Everyone looked at Peaches who was lying in Tina's arms, busily licking one of her fingers.

"Has Peaches met Cobweb, Freckle and Banjo yet?" Mandy asked, tickling the kitten's soft, apricot-coloured tummy.

"Not yet," replied Tina. "We decided to keep them away from each other until the kittens are feeling better."

"Talking of the kittens, I'd better go and make up their bottles," said Mrs Cunningham, and she hurried off to the kitchen.

"It was you who found the kittens, wasn't it, Mandy?" asked Alex. "Tina told us all about it."

Mandy nodded. "Yes, I heard one of them mewing when we were in the garden."

"Thank goodness you did," said Alex.

"They're gorgeous, aren't they? I was playing with Banjo and Freckle this morning. They're pretty lively considering they're still so young."

"Let's go into the kitchen and see them," suggested Tina. "I'd better leave Peaches in here, though."

She put Peaches on the sofa, and they all went out of the living-room. Mandy couldn't help laughing at the kitten's face. She looked very cross at being left behind!

Mrs Cunningham was at the worktop, whisking some yellow milk powder in a jug of warm water. She turned and smiled as everyone came in. "They're just waking up," she said.

Mandy and James bent eagerly over the cardboard box. Banjo and Freckle were already awake and mewing for attention, scrambling to get out of the box. Cobweb was still half-asleep and yawning.

"Oh, their eyes have opened!" Mandy said, delighted. "Look, Banjo's and Freckle's are green."

"This one's my favourite," said James, scooping up Banjo. "He's so naughty!" He waggled his fingers, and the kitten grabbed them and clung on like a little monkey.

"I love them all," said Tina, giving Freckle a cuddle.

"Come on, Cobweb." Mandy lightly tickled the kitten's grey head. "Are you going to wake up? It's time for your feed."

Cobweb yawned again, and slowly opened her blue eyes. Now that they were fully open, they looked huge, and sparkled like sapphires.

"She's so pretty, isn't she?" said Tina. "Can we feed them now, Mum?"

Mrs Hope and Mrs Cunningham handed out the bottles and Mandy, James and Tina sat down, each with a kitten in their lap. James had Banjo, Tina had Freckle and Mandy had Cobweb. Freckle and Banjo grabbed at the bottles, and began to suck greedily straightaway. But Cobweb didn't seem very interested, and she pulled away from the rubber teat after just a few mouthfuls.

"Come on, Cobweb," Mandy urged, trying gently to push the teat back into the kitten's mouth. "Have a bit more."

But the kitten turned her head away every time Mandy moved the bottle towards her. Feeling worried, Mandy looked over at her mum.

"We can't make her drink if she doesn't want to, love," Mrs Hope said softly. "Don't get too upset. Cobweb's weaker than her brothers, but she'll probably pick up over the next couple of days."

"I hope so," Mandy whispered, stroking the tiny kitten's back. "I really hope so."

6

Lily's special secret

"Oh, Jean, the kittens are gorgeous," Mandy exclaimed, as she leaned against the receptionist's desk. "Cobweb's eyes are so big and blue."

"And we saw Tina today at school, and she said that they're fine," James added.

It was Monday, and James had come back to Animal Ark with Mandy after school. Mrs

Hope had promised to take them over to the Cunninghams' for a quick visit after she'd finished evening surgery. At playtime, everyone had been talking about the big surprise that was coming up at the Christmas party. Mandy and James hadn't breathed a word about the puppet show, but it was hard keeping such an exciting secret!

"It's marvellous that the kittens are getting on so well," said Jean, sorting through some files. "But what about Cobweb? I thought you were worried that she wasn't feeding properly?"

Mandy felt a pang of worry. "Tina said Cobweb's sleeping a lot, and she's still not drinking much milk."

"Well, hopefully she'll get her appetite back in a day or two," Jean said. "Isn't it quiet tonight?" she added, glancing round the empty waiting-room. "We've only got one more patient booked in. Still, I'm sure your mum and dad will be frantic enough over Christmas!"

Mandy nodded. Christmas was usually a busy time at Animal Ark because some people fed their pets too much rich food, and then they were sick.

At that moment the outside door was pushed open, and a man and a woman walked in carrying a cat basket. They came straight over to Jean's desk, looking rather worried.

"We're Mr and Mrs Devlin," said the man, resting the cat basket on the desk. "We've got an appointment to see the vet with our cat, Lily."

"Ah, yes, this is the first time you've visited us, isn't it?" said Jean.

Mrs Devlin nodded. She was young and very pretty, with curly dark hair. "That's right. We've only just moved to Welford."

Mandy couldn't resist peeping into the basket to take a look at Lily. She always loved meeting new animals! But what she saw gave her quite a shock. Lily was a young black cat, but her fur wasn't sleek and glossy. It looked matted and dirty, and she was very thin. She clawed miserably at the sides of the basket, letting out a yowl every so often. Mandy glanced at James. He was staring at

Lily too, and obviously wondering what was the matter with her.

"Can I just have your address, please?" asked Jean, picking up her pen.

"17, Willow Lane," replied Mr Devlin. Mandy wondered if they'd met the Cunninghams yet, who lived at number 21.

"Thank you," said Jean. "Do take a seat."

Mr Devlin was about to pick up the cat basket again when he noticed Mandy and James staring at Lily. "She doesn't look too good, does she?" he said sadly. "She went missing for about five or six days just after we moved here. She only came back home the day before yesterday."

"Oh, poor Lily," Mandy said.

Lily was scrabbling at the door of the cage, trying to get out of the basket. Suddenly, though, she seemed worn out, and she flopped down on her blanket with her head on her paws.

"We were so worried about her when she disappeared," Mrs Devlin chimed in, sitting down on one of the chairs. Mandy and James sat down next to her. "We thought she must have tried to go back to our old house. We couldn't believe it when she turned up on the doorstep!"

"So we've brought her in to make sure she's all right," her husband added. "She's lost so much weight, and she's just not herself."

Lily raised her head and let out another mournful howl.

"She absolutely hates being in the basket," Mrs Devlin told Mandy and James. She looked at Jean Knox. "Would you mind if we let her out?"

Jean smiled. "That sounds like a good idea," she said.

Mr Devlin opened up the basket, and Lily looked a little more cheerful. She padded her way out on to Mrs Devlin's lap and stretched over to sniff at Mandy. Instead of settling down on her owner's knees, she stepped on to Mandy's lap, turned round a few times and then lay down, purring very faintly.

"Well!" Mrs Devlin laughed. "Lily's really taken to you. I'm sorry, I don't know your name."

"I'm Mandy Hope," said Mandy, gently stroking Lily's thin back. The cat had closed her eyes, and looked as if she was already half-asleep. "And this is my friend James Hunter. My mum and dad are the vets here."

"Well, no wonder you're good with animals," Mr Devlin said with a smile. "Lily doesn't take to just anybody, you know!"

The door to the consulting-room opened and Mandy's mum came out. She looked rather surprised to see Mandy sitting there with a cat on her lap. "Hello, you must be the Devlins," she said, coming towards them. "And this must be Lily."

"She doesn't like being in the basket," Mr Devlin explained. "But she seems to like sitting on Mandy's lap."

"So I see!" smiled Emily Hope. "She looks so comfortable, I hardly like to disturb her. Mandy, would you carry Lily into the surgery, please? That's if Mr and Mrs Devlin don't mind?"

"Of course not," said Mrs Devlin, standing up.

Mandy picked up Lily and carried her

across the waiting-room. The cat hardly stirred, and her eyes stayed closed. She seemed so weak and tired. Mandy hoped that there was nothing seriously wrong with her.

As the Devlins and James followed Mandy into the treatment-room, Mr Devlin explained to Mrs Hope how they had lost and found their cat.

"We don't know where she's been for the last four or five days," he said. "But she obviously hasn't been eating much, as she's got so thin."

"I feel awful now because we actually put Lily on a diet a few weeks ago," said Mrs Devlin, biting her lip. "She was really getting quite tubby."

Mandy put Lily carefully down on the examining-table. The cat crouched there, blinking her green eyes, too weary to look round the room or sniff at the table.

"Poor Lily," said Mrs Hope gently. "She does look quite miserable, doesn't she? If you say she was getting fat just a few weeks ago, I wouldn't have expected her to be quite so thin now. Four or five days without food wouldn't make that much difference. Let's see if we can find out what's wrong with her."

After a few moments, Mrs Hope raised her head and looked at the Devlins. "I can tell you exactly why Lily was getting bigger a few weeks ago," she said. "She was expecting kittens!"

The Devlins gasped, and Mandy and James looked at each other in surprise.

"And I'd say she had the kittens about a week ago," Mandy's mum added.

"But Lily's hardly more than a kitten herself!" Mr Devlin exclaimed. "She's not even a year old."

"Cats can get pregnant from around six months old," Mrs Hope told him. "So Lily is just about old enough to have had her first litter."

Mrs Devlin was frowning and looking worried. "But if Lily *has* had kittens," she said, "where on earth could they be?"

Mandy's hand flew to her mouth as an idea suddenly popped into her head. Could it be the answer? Everything seemed to fit. "Mum!" she gasped. "Do you think Cobweb, Banjo and Freckle could be Lily's missing kittens?"

7

Cobweb in trouble

Mandy could hardly contain her excitement as she looked eagerly at her mum. Surely there was a good chance that the kittens might be Lily's? After all, the Cunninghams lived very close to the Devlins. Lily could easily have made her way into Tina's garden to have her kittens if she was lost.

"It's certainly possible," agreed Emily Hope.

"Well done, Mandy!" said James, patting her on the back.

The Devlins were looking completely confused.

"Does this mean you *know* where Lily's kittens are?" asked Mr Devlin.

Quickly Mandy explained how they'd found a litter of tiny kittens in Tina's garden, only two doors away from the Devlins' house.

"Of course, we can't be sure that they're Lily's kittens," Mandy's mum warned. "But it seems likely, I must say."

Mrs Devlin was looking very excited. "What colour are they?" she asked.

"Banjo's black, like Lily," replied James. "And Freckle is white with ginger bits."

"And Cobweb's a beautiful smoky grey tabby," Mandy added.

Mrs Devlin turned to her husband. "I know kittens don't always look like their parents," she said, "but Lily's mum was a silver tabby, which sounds just like Cobweb. Remember, David?"

Mr Devlin nodded. "They *must* be Lily's kittens," he said.

Mandy felt a thrill of excitement run through her, and she gave James a look of delight. They'd found the kittens' mum!

"I wonder why Lily abandoned her babies, though," Mr Devlin went on, sounding puzzled.

"She probably didn't mean to," replied Mrs Hope. "She might have gone looking for food for herself, and then realised that she was close to home. And I suppose once you got her back, you didn't let her out again, so she couldn't return to the kittens even if she wanted to."

"That's right," Mr Devlin agreed. "She looked so thin and ill that we couldn't bear to let her out into the snow."

"Poor Lily. She must have been desperate to get back to her babies." Mrs Devlin stroked her cat's head and glanced at Mandy. "Are the kittens doing all right without their mum?"

"Banjo and Freckle are fine," Mandy replied. "But Cobweb was the smallest and she's still a bit weak. She's not feeding very well either."

"Oh, dear." Mrs Devlin looked worried. "David, we'd better collect the kittens from the Cunninghams right away and take them home with us. Maybe Cobweb will get better when she's back with her mum again."

"I'm afraid that might not be a good idea, Mrs Devlin," Emily Hope broke in.

Mandy looked at her mum in surprise, wondering what she was going to say. Surely it was *much* better for Cobweb to be back with Lily?

"Lily hasn't been eating enough over the last few weeks, partly because she was on a diet and partly because she got lost," Mandy's mum continued. "That means she isn't making any milk, so she won't be able to feed the kittens herself."

Mandy felt bitterly disappointed.

"Oh, dear." Mr Devlin looked disappointed too. "Well, can't Ruth and I feed the kittens, like the Cunninghams are doing?"

"Yes, of course," Mandy's mum agreed. "But they need frequent regular feeds, so one of you will have to be at home all the time."

The Devlins looked at each other. "Hmm, that wouldn't be easy," said David Devlin with a frown. "You see, we both work all day."

"Well, maybe the Cunninghams wouldn't mind keeping the kittens, just for the next few weeks," Mandy's mum suggested. "I could ask them, if you like."

Mandy's face lit up as the Devlins nodded gratefully.

"It would be very kind of them," said Mr Devlin. "And we could always pop round and give them a hand in the evenings and at weekends."

"Do you think they'd mind if we visited them right now?" asked Mrs Devlin. "I'm dying to see Lily's babies!"

"We're going over there now ourselves," said Mrs Hope. "Would you like to come with us? I could introduce you to the Cunninghams, and then we can decide together what to do about the kittens."

Mr Devlin frowned. "What are we going to do if the Cunninghams *can't* keep them?" he asked.

"Let's wait and see," said Mrs Hope sensibly. "Meanwhile, I'd like to keep Lily here for a couple of days so I can put her on a drip. That will help to build up her strength again. And perhaps you should think about making sure Lily doesn't have any more kittens. The operation is very straightforward."

"Just tell us when Lily's well enough, and she can have the operation at once," said Mrs Devlin.

"You could also consider having her microchipped," Mrs Hope added. "Then you're much more likely to get her back if she goes missing again."

James turned to Mandy as Mrs Hope picked up Lily to take her into the residential unit. "Isn't this *brilliant*?" he said happily. "I can't wait to tell Tina. She's going to be so pleased that we've found the kittens' mum."

Mandy nodded. "I know," she agreed. "I just wish Lily was well enough to feed Cobweb, though. Then she might have started getting better and putting on weight."

James's face fell. "I hadn't thought of that. Maybe she'll be OK anyway."

"I hope so," Mandy replied.

Mrs Hope carried Lily through to the large room at the back of the surgery where overnight patients were housed. Mandy, James and the Devlins watched as Mrs Hope settled Lily in a large, comfortable cage and attached a drip to her front leg. Lily seemed sleepy again, and her green eyes were already closing as everyone tiptoed out of the room.

"She's going to be fine," said Mrs Hope. "Now, shall we go over to the Cunninghams'?"

Everyone put on their coats, and they set off through the village. It was a dark and frosty night, and stars twinkled overhead. There were brightly-lit Christmas trees in the living-room window of almost every house, and some people had strung fairy lights on the trees in their front gardens. Mandy had almost forgotten about Christmas in the excitement over the kittens, but now she thought that the best present of all would be if Cobweb started getting better.

"We'll have to think about finding new homes for the kittens when they're old enough," said Mrs Devlin, turning to her husband as they crossed the village green.

"James and I could help," Mandy offered. "We could put up posters in Animal Ark, and at school."

"Thank you. What a good idea," smiled Mrs Devlin.

They arrived at the Cunninghams' house and Mrs Hope rang the bell. Tina answered

the door with Peaches tucked under her arm. She looked surprised to see so many people on the doorstep.

"Tina, we've got some good news," Mandy announced. "We've found the kittens' mum!"

"Oh!" Tina's face broke into a huge smile, and she hugged Peaches close to her. The kitten began to purr loudly as if she was pleased too. "That's great. Where is she?"

Before anyone could answer, Tina's mum came out of the kitchen and hurried down the hall towards them. "Did I hear someone say that you'd found the kittens' mother?" she asked.

Mr Devlin stepped forward. "Hello, Mrs Cunningham," he said. "I'm David Devlin, and my wife and I have just moved into number 17. It looks like it was our cat, Lily, who had the kittens."

"Thank you so much for looking after them," his wife added.

"Not at all!" Mrs Cunningham exclaimed. "They're adorable. Come in out of the cold, and tell us all about it."

Everyone trooped into the hall and began pulling off their outdoor clothes. As Mr and Mrs Devlin explained about Lily and how they'd lost her, Tina turned to Mandy, looking a bit disappointed. "I guess the kittens will be going home then," she said quietly. "I'm really going to miss them, especially Cobweb."

Mandy glanced over at her mum, who'd heard what Tina was saying.

"Well, we have a problem because the kittens can't go home just yet," Emily Hope said. Quickly she explained to Tina and Mrs Cunningham that Lily didn't have any milk to feed the kittens, and the Devlins were out at work all day so it would be difficult for them to feed the kittens by hand.

"That's all right," Mrs Cunningham said immediately. "We'll just keep them here for the moment, shall we?"

Mandy and James both grinned at the delighted look on Tina's face.

"We'd be really grateful," said Mr Devlin. "We can always come round and help out when we're at home."

"And we can see that you're very good with cats!" Mrs Devlin added, looking down at Peaches who was lying cosily in Tina's arms. "What's this gorgeous kitten called? She's much too big to be one of Lily's!"

"This is Peaches," Tina said shyly.

Mandy smiled as Mrs Devlin tickled Peaches under the chin and the kitten immediately gave her fingers a good lick.

"Come through to the kitchen and see the kittens," said Tina's mum. "They're awake at the moment. Well, Banjo and Freckle are."

"How's Cobweb?" Mandy asked.

Tina looked worried. "She sleeps nearly all the time," she replied.

"Is she drinking more milk yet?" said James.

"Not really," sighed Tina. "Uncle Matt tried to feed her this morning, and she only had a few drops."

They all went into the kitchen, where Matt and Alex were lying on the floor playing with Banjo and Freckle. They held pieces of string which they were dangling over the kittens' heads, and Banjo and Freckle were trying to grab them. Tina put Peaches down on the floor, and she immediately dashed over to join in the fun.

"Matt, Alex, this is Mr and Mrs Devlin from number 17," said Tina's mum. "They think that the kittens belong to their cat, Lily."

"Oh, really?" Alex beamed. "We think they're lovely. We've been playing with them almost all day, haven't we, Matt?"

Tina's uncle nodded.

"They are gorgeous, aren't they?" said Mrs Devlin. "This one looks just like Lily." And she picked up Banjo and gave him a cuddle.

"Banjo and Freckle love Peaches," Tina smiled, as Freckle and Peaches began to chase each other around the table legs.

"What about Cobweb?" asked James.

"I've kept Peaches away from her so far," Tina replied. "Cobweb's so tiny, I'm scared Peaches might hurt her if she tries to play with her."

Mandy looked around for the little grey kitten. Cobweb was curled up in a tight, fluffy ball in the box, fast asleep. Mrs Cunningham had cut down the sides of the box so that the kittens could get in and out when they wanted, but Cobweb was obviously happy to stay where she was.

"Hello, Cobweb." Mandy knelt down by the box and gently touched the kitten's ears. "How are you feeling?"

Cobweb opened her big, blue eyes very slowly and lifted her head to stare at Mandy. Then she gave a little mew and curled up into a ball again.

"She doesn't want to get out of the box, or play, or do anything," Tina said sadly, keeping a tight hold on Peaches. The bigger kitten was staring curiously down at Cobweb and struggling impatiently to get out of Tina's arms.

Mr and Mrs Devlin came over to join Mandy and Tina. "Poor little thing," Mrs Devlin said quietly. She reached down and stroked Cobweb's soft grey coat, but the kitten didn't move. "I hope she'll be all right."

"So do I," Tina said in a wobbly voice.

Mandy could see that she was very upset. She'd obviously grown really fond of Cobweb. Mandy sighed, feeling very miserable. They all loved the little kitten, but there didn't seem to be anything they could do for her. How *could* they help Cobweb?

8

Peaches to the rescue

"Only two days to go to the puppet show
and the party!" chanted James. "I can't
wait. It's really hard not being able to tell
everyone about it. Ow!" He jumped as
Banjo pounced on his foot. "Let go of my
laces, Banjo!"

Mandy laughed. "He's such a pickle!" She
glanced over at the box in the corner, where

Cobweb was asleep again, and sighed. "Not like Cobweb."

It was Tuesday afternoon, and Mandy and James had walked home with Tina after school to see the kittens again. Mandy had hoped that Cobweb would have cheered up a bit since the Devlins' visit the day before. But Tina told her that Cobweb was just the same, and that she'd hardly had any milk for breakfast. Mandy was getting more and more worried about the poorly little kitten. She, James and Tina had put up a poster at school asking if anyone could give the kittens new homes, but it didn't look like Cobweb would be well enough to leave the Cunninghams for a long time yet.

"Are Matt and Alex rehearsing *Cinderella* tonight?" James asked Tina.

"No, they've gone to see some friends in Walton," replied Tina. "They won't be back till late."

"Don't look so disappointed, James," laughed Mrs Cunningham. "You'll be able to see the show very soon."

"Mum and Dad are busy this evening, so

Gran's coming to collect me and James," Mandy told Tina's mum. "She'll be here about half-past five."

Tina's mum glanced at the clock. "Then we've just got time to feed the kittens before you go," she said.

"Oh, good," Mandy said. Maybe today would be the day when Cobweb finally started to feed properly. It would be lovely to see her running round and getting into mischief, just like Banjo and Freckle.

"Let's wake Cobweb up," said Tina, as her mum began to make up the bottles of milk.

Mandy, James and Tina knelt down beside the box and Mandy ruffled the kitten's grey fur with her finger. "Come on, Cobweb," she said. "Time for your dinner."

Banjo and Freckle were already sitting at Mrs Cunningham's feet, mewing loudly. They knew it was suppertime! But Cobweb didn't seem to care. She blinked her blue eyes and stayed exactly where she was.

"No, Peaches," scolded Tina as the apricot-coloured kitten padded forward

to nose curiously at Cobweb. "Leave Cobweb alone. She's much too small to play with you."

"Shall I put Peaches in the living-room?" asked James.

"Oh, thank you," said Tina, and she handed her kitten to James. "Peaches always wants to drink the milk if she stays in here at feeding-time!"

Mandy sat down at the table with Cobweb on her lap. The kitten was so tiny, she hardly weighed a thing. Tina was already feeding

Banjo, and James hurried back into the kitchen to feed Freckle, who seemed almost as hungry as his brother. But it took Mandy ages to coax Cobweb into opening her mouth so that she could pop the bottle in. Even then, the kitten only took a few sips before she stopped, mewing weakly.

"Keep trying, Mandy," Mrs Cunningham urged.

"Come on, Cobweb," Mandy said gently. "Look, your brothers have nearly finished their bottles."

"Freckle *has* finished," said James.

"So has Banjo," added Tina, holding up the empty bottle.

Mandy did her best, but Cobweb only sucked down a couple more drops of milk before she pulled away from the bottle again and stared round at everyone with big, worried eyes.

"Maybe Cobweb would feel better if there weren't so many people watching her," Tina suggested. "James, let's take Freckle and Banjo into the living-room to play with Peaches."

"OK," James agreed, and they disappeared down the hall, each with a kitten in their arms.

"I'm really worried about Cobweb," Mandy said anxiously to Mrs Cunningham. "Maybe my mum should have another look at her."

Before Mrs Cunningham could answer, Peaches bounded through the kitchen door, looking very pleased with herself. She spotted Cobweb on Mandy's lap, and, before anyone could stop her, she jumped up, right next to the tiny grey kitten.

"Peaches!" Mandy gasped, taken by surprise.

A second later, Tina and James appeared in the kitchen doorway.

"Peaches, you bad girl!" Tina scolded. "Sorry, Mandy. She was waiting by the living-room door, and she ran out when we went in with Freckle and Banjo."

"Don't let her frighten Cobweb," said Tina's mum.

But Mandy stared down at the two kittens on her lap and shook her head. "Peaches isn't frightening Cobweb," she said softly. "Look!"

Peaches was gently licking the little kitten, smoothing down the fluffy grey fur with her rasping pink tongue. Cobweb was sitting quietly, gazing up at the bigger kitten and purring more loudly than any of them had ever heard before.

"Oh!" Tina gasped. "Do you think Peaches knows that Cobweb isn't very well? Maybe that's why she's licking her, just like Peaches' mum used to lick *her*."

"And Cobweb seems to like it!" said James. "She doesn't look so miserable now."

"I'll try her with the milk again," Mandy decided. While Peaches carried on grooming Cobweb, Mandy slipped the teat into the kitten's mouth. For once, Cobweb didn't try to pull away. She started drinking the milk, and this time she kept on feeding.

"Look!" Mandy said in delight, holding up the bottle a few minutes later. "Cobweb's drunk nearly all of it."

"Thanks to Peaches," Tina added proudly, picking up her kitten and giving her a big

hug. "Cobweb loves getting kissed by her!"

"Well done, Peaches," said James.

Cobweb gave a huge yawn, showing her pink mouth and all her tiny white teeth. Mandy laid her gently back in the kittens' box. Tina put Peaches down on the floor, and the kitten immediately bounded over to the box and climbed in beside Cobweb.

Cobweb gave a pleased chirrup and the two kittens curled up together in one furry ball. As soon as they were settled, Peaches began to wash Cobweb's ears and face, licking up any stray drops of milk.

"I think Cobweb's going to be OK, don't you?" Mandy said, feeling very relieved. "She's got Peaches to look after her now."

"Thank goodness!" said James. "Tina, what about Freckle and Banjo? Shall I go and see how they're doing?"

"Oh, yes, please," said Tina. "I'd almost forgotten about them! We shouldn't have left them on their own, really."

"Don't worry, I'll go and make sure they're OK." James went off down the hall.

Mandy gazed at Cobweb and Peaches, and

smiled as she watched both kittens' eyes close peacefully. Cobweb was lucky to have a special friend like Peaches, who knew what it felt like to need lots of extra kisses.

Suddenly there was the sound of running footsteps out in the hall. A moment later James appeared in the kitchen doorway. He looked round at everyone, his eyes wide in alarm. "Come quick!" he gasped. "Banjo and Freckle have caught a mouse!"

9

Mouse alert!

"What?" Mandy cried, jumping to her feet.

"A mouse?" repeated Mrs Cunningham. "We don't have any mice in this house."

"Are you sure, James?" asked Tina. "Banjo and Freckle aren't much bigger than a mouse themselves!"

"Come and see," replied James, turning and hurrying back to the living-room.

Mandy, Tina and Mrs Cunningham followed him quickly. James rushed over to the sofa and pointed behind it. "Look!"

The sofa was pushed against the wall, leaving a very narrow gap. Mandy bent down and peered into the space. It was very dark in there, but she could just see Freckle and Banjo playing with a small, white, furry thing with pink ears.

"It looks like a mouse," Tina breathed, staring over Mandy's shoulder.

"We'd better move the sofa and get rid of it," Mrs Cunningham said grimly.

But before they could do anything, Banjo grabbed the mouse in his teeth and ran out from behind the sofa. Freckle followed, mewing crossly.

"Don't let them get away!" James called anxiously. "The mouse might still be alive."

Banjo dropped the mouse proudly at Mandy's feet. Mandy crouched down to look closely at it and burst out laughing.

"What's so funny?" asked James.

Mandy picked up the mouse and held it

out. "It's all right," she said with a grin. "It's not real. It's a toy mouse!"

"Thank goodness for that," said James, grinning back.

"Oh, no!" gasped Tina, gazing at the soggy, furry mess. "It's one of Uncle Matt's puppets! They've got two mice that they turn into white horses to pull Cinderella's coach."

"Oh, dear. This one doesn't look like it could pull a coach now," said James.

They all stared down at the puppet. It had been thoroughly chewed, and the kittens' sharp little claws had torn the cloth body in several places. One of its beady black eyes and both its ears were hanging on by the merest threads.

"It's all my fault," Tina said miserably. "I shouldn't have left Freckle and Banjo in here on their own."

"Don't worry, love." Her mum put an arm round her. "I'm sure it can be fixed." She frowned at the torn puppet. "It looks quite bad, though. And Matt and Alex won't be back until late tonight, which doesn't leave them much time to mend it."

Mandy realised that Mrs Cunningham was right. The puppet would have to be mended very cleverly or the stitches would show when it was on stage. She hoped Matt and Alex could sort it out before the show.

Suddenly the doorbell rang.

"That'll probably be your gran, Mandy," said Tina's mum, glancing at the clock. She went out into the hall, and came back with Grandma Hope.

"Hello, you two." Gran smiled at Mandy and James. "Hello, Tina." Then she spotted Banjo and Freckle who were playing hide and seek under the hearthrug. "Are these the famous kittens I've been hearing about?"

Mandy nodded. "And they've been really naughty, Gran," she said, holding out the mouse. "They've chewed up one of Tina's uncle's puppets! And the show is only two days away—" Suddenly Mandy stopped. If there was one person who could sew anything back together, it was her gran!

"Oh, dear." Gran took the mouse and examined it closely. "This poor fellow's going to need quite a bit of work, isn't he?"

"Gran," Mandy began, "do you think *you* could fix him? It's really important, or Cinderella won't have *two* white horses to pull her golden coach!"

Her gran started to laugh. "Well, I don't know much about mice, but I'll have a go," she said.

Tina's face lit up. "Oh, that would be great, Mrs Hope!" she said.

"It's very kind of you, Dorothy," said Mrs Cunningham gratefully. "I know Matt and Alex will be really pleased."

"Well, the show must go on!" said Mandy's gran, her eyes twinkling. "I'll have it ready by tomorrow."

"Thanks, Gran!" said Mandy, giving her a big hug.

"Lily looks a lot better, doesn't she?" Mandy said to James. It was Wednesday afternoon. Mandy and James had just arrived at Animal Ark after school, and they had headed straight to the residential unit at the back of the surgery. Mandy's mum had said that Lily could go home today, and the Devlins had come to collect her. They were in the consulting-room, talking to Mrs Hope.

"She looks great," agreed James.

Lily was looking much healthier after two days on a drip. Her coat was glossy and her eyes were much brighter. She seemed livelier, too. She padded over to the front of the cage, purring softly, and rubbed her head against Mandy and James's fingers.

"When are we going over to Tina's?" asked James.

"After the Devlins have taken Lily," Mandy replied. "We mustn't forget to pick up the mouse from Gran on the way."

"I wonder if she's managed to fix it," said James.

"If anyone can, Gran can," Mandy promised him with a grin.

Mrs Hope came in at that moment with the Devlins close behind her. Mr Devlin was carrying Lily's basket. He and his wife beamed when they saw how much better Lily looked.

"She's almost back to her old self, isn't she?" said Mrs Devlin, stroking Lily's ear through the bars of the cage. "Thank goodness!"

"Are you ready to come home now, Lily?" Mr Devlin asked, putting the basket on the floor and opening the door.

Mrs Hope unlatched the cage, and Mandy and James laughed as Lily ran straight into her basket.

"That's the first time she's ever got into her basket without being pushed!" said Mrs Devlin. "Usually she hates it."

"She knows she's going home," said Mrs Hope with a smile. "Now, if you talk to Jean before you go, you can make an appointment for Lily to have her operation straight after Christmas. That will make sure she doesn't have any more unexpected litters of kittens! We'll microchip her then, too."

The Devlins nodded.

"Goodbye, Lily," Mandy said, watching the black cat settle down happily on her blanket. "Now just make sure you don't get lost again!"

"Gran, it's perfect!" Mandy stared hard at the mouse puppet in her hand, but she couldn't see where the eye and ears had been sewn back on. Gran's invisible mending had done the trick. "Look, James." She popped the mouse puppet on to her finger, and wiggled it at him.

"It's brilliant, Mrs Hope," said James admiringly.

"I washed it, too," said Gran, "so it's nice and fluffy again."

"This mouse is going to be the star of the show!" Mandy declared. "Thanks, Gran."

"We'd better get the puppet back to Matthew and Alex, in case they're having a last-minute rehearsal," said Mrs Hope. "Come on, you two."

Grandma Hope saw them to the door, and waved as they went off down the path. "Enjoy the party," she called. "I've made some cakes and biscuits for you, and I'll be dropping them off at the school tomorrow."

"Thanks, Gran," Mandy said, waving back.

"I wonder how Cobweb and Peaches are getting on?" said James as they walked the short distance to Willow Lane.

"Well, Tina said that Cobweb drank quite a lot of milk again this morning, while Peaches was licking her ears, of course!" Mandy said happily. "Isn't it brilliant, Mum? Peaches is really looking after Cobweb."

"It sounds like it's just what Cobweb needs," her mum agreed.

They arrived at the Cunninghams' house and James rang the bell. No one came for a few moments, and James was just about to ring it again when the door suddenly opened.

Matt stood in the doorway, looking worried. "Hi, come in," he said. "Sorry, we're in a bit of a mess at the moment. You won't believe this, but we've lost one of our mouse puppets!"

Mandy grinned at him. "No, you haven't," she said, taking the puppet out of the carrier bag Gran had wrapped it in. "Didn't Tina tell you? We took it away so my gran could mend it."

"Oh, yes, we heard all about *that*," said Matt. He took the puppet and looked at it closely. "Your gran's done a great job, Mandy. Please give her a big thank you from us."

"So what do you mean, you've lost a mouse puppet?" James asked curiously.

"I mean, we've lost the *other* one!" Matt groaned.

Mandy, James, and Mrs Hope stared at

him. "Oh no!" Mandy gasped.

Matt led Mandy, James and Mrs Hope inside. Tina, Mrs Cunningham and Alex were frantically searching the living-room. Tina and her mum were looking behind the sofa and armchairs while Alex was sorting through a big box of puppets. Dragons, witches and wizards lay on the carpet. Banjo and Freckle were scampering everywhere, weaving in and out of people's legs and having a great time.

"Shall we help you look?" offered James.

"Oh, please do," Alex sighed. "I don't know what we're going to do if we can't find this mouse. We don't have time to make another one."

"Where are Cobweb and Peaches?" Mandy asked Tina.

"In the box in the kitchen," replied Tina.

"I'll just go and say hello," Mandy said. "Then I'll help you search for the puppet."

She hurried off to the kitchen and peeped round the door, not wanting to disturb the kittens if they were asleep. But Cobweb and Peaches were both awake. They were sitting

bolt upright in the box, staring down at a small, white, furry thing with pink ears.

"Oh!" Mandy couldn't help smiling. "It's the missing mouse puppet!"

As Mandy watched, Peaches put out a paw and gently patted the mouse. Then she nudged it towards Cobweb. Cobweb immediately grabbed the mouse with her paw and began to sniff it.

Mandy burst out laughing. "I've found the mouse!" she called.

Everyone came dashing down the hall, and arrived in the kitchen just as Mandy rescued the puppet from the two kittens. Luckily, it hadn't been chewed or damaged at all.

"Peaches!" scolded Tina, trying to sound stern. "Did *you* take the mouse?"

Peaches began to purr loudly, not looking the least bit ashamed.

"Don't be too cross, Tina," Mandy said with a grin. "I think Peaches is just trying to get Cobweb to play. She's the best kitten nurse ever!"

10

New homes for Christmas

"I'm full," declared James, pushing away his paper plate and patting his tummy. "I can't eat another thing!"

"Oh, aren't you going to have one of Gran's choc-chip buns?" Mandy said, pointing to a laden plate. "She made them especially for me to bring to the party."

"Well, maybe just one," said James,

pushing up his silver party hat which had fallen over one eye.

Mandy and Tina laughed. James had already eaten four sausage rolls, six sandwiches and three mince pies, not to mention several handfuls of crisps!

"Look, I think those are our stars hanging up over there," said Tina, nudging Mandy and pointing up at the ceiling.

Mandy nodded, and glanced around the school hall in delight. She thought it was the best Christmas party she'd ever been to. Every corner of the hall had been decorated by Mrs Cunningham and the other members of the PTA. A lofty Christmas tree stood in one corner, and at the far end of the hall was the puppet theatre, covered with a sparkly purple sheet so you couldn't tell what it was. Everyone in the hall was very excited, wondering what was going to happen, and Mandy, James and Tina had found it very hard not to let the secret out.

Once everyone had finished eating, Mrs Garvie, the headteacher, stood in front of the covered theatre and smiled warmly.

"And now for our surprise!" she announced. "I'd like you all to welcome *The Perfect Puppeteers.*"

Everyone gasped and clapped loudly. Mandy, James and Tina grinned at each other as Matt and Alex appeared from behind the theatre in matching black outfits and pulled off the sheet with a dramatic flourish.

"Hello, Welford Primary School!" said Matt, with a low bow.

"Hello," the audience called excitedly.

Matt cupped a hand to his ear and frowned. "I didn't hear that, did you, Alex?" he said. "I thought we had an audience here somewhere!"

Alex shook her head. "I didn't hear anything either. Maybe they've all gone home!"

"Let's try again," Matt suggested, his eyes twinkling. "Hello, Welford Primary School!"

"HELLO!" This time everyone in the hall, including the teachers, joined in. The noise was deafening.

"Ah, that's better," said Alex with a grin.

"*The Perfect Puppeteers* would like to invite you to a performance of *Cinderella*. Prepare to be amazed and astounded!"

The audience clapped even harder, as Matt and Alex disappeared behind the puppet theatre again. Then, with a fanfare of trumpets blaring from a cassette machine, the show began. Cinderella popped up, wearing a dress of colourful rags. She started sweeping the kitchen and got told off by the two Ugly Sisters for not doing it properly. Her friend, Buttons, appeared beside her to sing a song to cheer her up.

The show was very funny, especially the Ugly Sister puppets. One wore a red wig which flew off every time she got angry, and the other had big round eyes which popped right out of her head.

Mandy, James and Tina were on the edge of their seats as they watched out for the scene when the Fairy Godmother had to get Cinderella ready for the ball. They couldn't wait to see the mice! When the Fairy Godmother waved her wand, and said, "Bring me two white mice," they held their breath and nudged each other.

Mandy stared hard at the two mice as they scampered on to the stage. It wasn't easy to tell which mouse was the one that Gran had mended, but then Mandy smiled to herself. One mouse's eyes were wider apart, making him look slightly surprised. Mandy guessed that *that* was the one Gran had mended. She must have sewn the eye back on a tiny bit further over than it should be.

James seemed to have spotted exactly the same thing. "I think that surprised-looking

mouse is the one your gran mended," he whispered.

"Wouldn't *you* look surprised if you were going to be turned into a horse?" Mandy laughed as, with a puff of glittering smoke, the two mice disappeared and a pair of beautiful white horses took their place.

Mandy, James and Tina were also keen to see the scene where the smoke bomb was let off and the pumpkin changed into a coach. Even though they knew how it was done, they gasped along with the rest of the audience as smoke filled the stage and the pumpkin vanished, to be quickly replaced by the gleaming golden coach.

"They're brilliant, aren't they?" James whispered to Mandy, as the audience clapped loudly. Mandy nodded, too busy watching the show to reply.

There was more applause as Cinderella changed from her rags into a beautiful silver dress and went off to the ball. Buttons was left behind in the kitchen and he sang another song, this time with the audience's help. Alex came out to pin the words to the front of the puppet theatre. The song was full of tongue-twisters, and soon everyone was laughing so much they could hardly get the words out. At the end of the song, Buttons started throwing sweets into the audience, and everyone scrambled to get one.

"Look out, Tina!" Mandy grinned, catching a toffee as it flew towards them.

The final scene was the wedding of Cinderella and the Prince, and there were loud cheers as Cinderella appeared in her white wedding dress to take a bow.

"That was great!" said James, clapping as hard as he could.

"I think everyone liked it, didn't they?" said Tina, looking round the hall at all the smiling faces.

"Of course they did!" Mandy replied.

Matt and Alex appeared from behind the theatre for one last time, and bowed to the audience.

"Thank you very much," said Matt. "We're really glad you enjoyed the show."

"Now *we* want to say a special thank you,"

Alex added. "If it wasn't for some good friends of ours, we wouldn't have had any white mice in the show today. And then how would Cinderella have got to the ball? So Mandy, James and Tina, thank you!"

"It was great, Gran," Mandy said, as she, James and Grandma Hope walked through Welford. Gran had come to pick them up after the party and to collect her cake tins. "The mouse looked lovely, didn't he, James?"

James nodded. "And it was really funny, Mrs Hope," he told her. "One of the Ugly Sisters wore a wig which kept whizzing off, and once it landed on Mrs Garvie's lap!"

"The food was brilliant," Mandy added. "And then we had party games after the puppet show."

Gran laughed. "You won't be wanting any tea then," she said as they turned into Willow Lane.

"Well, maybe just a snack," Mandy said, grinning at James who was looking disappointed.

As they walked past the Cunninghams' house towards Lilac Cottage, the door flew open and Tina rushed out. She was red in the face and looked very excited. "Mandy! James!" she called. "I'm glad I saw you. I've got something really brilliant to tell you!"

"What is it?" asked James.

"Come inside and I'll tell you," Tina said, beaming.

"You got home quickly," Mandy remarked, as they walked up to the front door.

"Uncle Matt and Alex brought me home in their van with all the puppet stuff," Tina explained. "Come in."

Feeling very curious, Mandy and James went into the living-room, followed by Mandy's gran. The room was as cosy and welcoming as ever, with the Christmas tree twinkling in the corner. Mrs Cunningham was sitting on the sofa, and Matt and Alex were on their knees in front of the fire, playing with Banjo and Freckle. They were dangling a bit of silver tinsel over the kittens' heads, and Banjo and Freckle were trying to grab it. Peaches and Cobweb were curled up in front of the fire, purring, and as usual Peaches was giving the grey kitten a good wash.

"Mum and Dad have said that I can keep Cobweb!" Tina burst out, her eyes shining. "They said that she and Peaches get on so well, it would be a shame to split them up."

"That's great!" Mandy gasped. She'd been worrying about finding the right home for fragile little Cobweb, but now the problem was solved.

"And guess what?" Alex chimed in. "Matt and I have fallen in love with these two." She pointed at Freckle and Banjo. "And we're going to keep them! We've spoken to the Devlins, and they're really happy about it."

Mandy beamed and turned to James. "It looks like we can take those posters down now. The kittens have all got new homes!"

At that moment the doorbell rang and Mrs Cunningham went to see who it was. She came back with the Devlins, who were carrying three wicker cat baskets and three bright red tartan blankets.

"Hello, everyone," smiled Mr Devlin. "We thought we'd bring round a little Christmas present for the kittens – and their new owners! Look, new baskets and blankets for all of them."

"Let's see if they like them," said Mrs Devlin, putting the baskets down and tucking the blankets inside. Everyone watched as Banjo and Freckle jumped into two of the baskets and began to explore every corner, sniffing eagerly with their tails held straight up like tiny flags. Cobweb was a bit more wary, but after Peaches had given her a gentle nudge with her nose, she climbed into the third basket and settled down with her paws tucked underneath her.

"I think they like them!" said Tina.

Peaches looked rather put out that *she* didn't have a basket too. She padded over to Cobweb's basket, sniffed at it, then squeezed in next to the grey kitten. It was a bit of a tight fit, but neither kitten seemed to mind. They snuggled down together, curling their

bodies around each other. Peaches began to purr loudly, and licked Cobweb's ears.

"Merry Christmas, Peaches," Mandy laughed, kneeling down by the basket to stroke her. "And it looks like your kitten kisses have made it a really merry Christmas for Cobweb, too!"

Spaniel
Surprise

Spaniel Surprise

Special thanks to Narinder Dhami

Text copyright © 2000 Working Partners Ltd
Created by Working Partners Ltd, London W6 0QT
Original series created by Ben M. Baglio
Illustrations copyright © 1998 Paul Howard

First published as a single volume in Great Britain in 2000
by Hodder Children's Books

1

Give a Dog a Home

"Quick, James! It's almost time!" Mandy Hope flew into the living-room and hurried over to the TV. Pushing her fair hair out of her eyes, she switched the TV on, then turned impatiently to see what had happened to her best friend, James Hunter. "*James!*"

"Sorry!" James hurried into the room a few

249

seconds later, carrying his Labrador pup, Blackie, in his arms. "Blackie spotted a spider, and was chasing it around the kitchen!"

"Bad boy, Blackie!" Mandy said, but she was smiling as she petted the puppy's sleek head. "Now, you *are* going to sit quietly and let us watch our favourite programme, aren't you?"

"Blackie never sits quietly — except when he's asleep!" James sighed, putting the puppy down. As if he'd heard what James said, Blackie immediately yawned widely, and went to curl

up on the rug in front of the Hopes' fire. Mandy and James looked at each other and laughed.

"Your dad's gone into the surgery to check on the overnight patients." Mandy's mother, Emily Hope, came in carrying a cup of coffee. "We've got quite a few, so he might be some time."

Mandy's parents were both vets, and their surgery, Animal Ark, was attached to the stone cottage where the family lived. Mandy was mad about animals, and knew most of the pets in the village of Welford, where she lived. She couldn't wait until she was twelve, when she would be allowed to help her parents in the surgery.

"Oh, is Dad going to miss *Give a Dog a Home*?" Mandy asked anxiously. "Shall we tape it for him?"

Mrs Hope nodded. "Good idea. I know he enjoys it."

"And then we can watch it again ourselves if we want to!" James pointed out.

Mandy grinned as she went over to the video

251

recorder to put a tape in. There were lots of animal programmes on TV and she and James watched most of them, but *Give a Dog a Home* was their absolute favourite. Each programme focused on a particular dog who needed a new owner, and viewers were invited to ring in and offer the dog a good home. The dogs were usually strays that were in poor condition, and often mistreated. Mandy and James were always thrilled to see the difference after the programme's "TLC Squad" had lavished lots of tender, loving care on them.

"Your father said he's going to pick up the Christmas tree tomorrow," Mrs Hope remarked, as she settled herself in a comfy armchair. "So you'll have to help me get the box of decorations down from the loft, Mandy."

"Oh, great!" Mandy exclaimed, as she put a blank video into the machine. It wasn't long now until Christmas. In fact, they only had two more days left at school before term ended.

"Quick, Mandy! It's starting!" James said, as the familiar theme tune began, accompanied by shots of some of the dogs who were housed in the *Give a Dog a Home* kennel near York. Mandy pressed "record" and hurried back to her seat on the sofa, next to James. They were doubly excited because tonight was the beginning of a new series. The programme had been off the air for the last few months, and Mandy and James had been longing for it to come back.

"Hello, and welcome to a new series of *Give a Dog a Home!*" The presenter, Fiona Ramsay, a young, red-haired woman in jeans and a leather jacket, was standing outside the kennel entrance, smiling into the camera. "We've got a packed programme for you tonight, including updates on the dogs who were rehomed in our last series."

The picture changed to show a fully grown Dalmatian trotting quietly along a street, a young, dark-haired man holding her lead.

"Oh, that's Tina, the dotty Dalmatian!" Mandy exclaimed in delight.

"Yes, do you remember how lively she was?" James said. "They were afraid her new owner might find her too much of a handful," James added. "But she looks OK, doesn't she?"

Mandy nodded, her eyes shining. She loved it when animals who had been written off were successfully rehomed.

"Later we'll be talking to dog psychologist Dr Richard Lacey about what you can do if your pet is becoming aggressive," Fiona Ramsay went on. "We'll also be weighing up the merits of dried dog food versus canned, and we'll be conducting some tests with the help of some of our canine friends from the *Give a Dog a Home* kennels! But first . . ."

The camera zoomed in closer as the presenter's smile faded, and she became more serious. "*Give a Dog a Home* is all about finding new homes for very special pups. And, with Christmas coming up, we all know about the problem of unwanted pets. But we have a very touching story for you tonight, about one little dog's search for a loving owner."

Mandy and James watched intently as Fiona Ramsay's face faded from the screen, and a picture of the kennel's reception area flashed up instead. The TLC squad, Lynn, Mel and Andy, were there. Lynn and Andy were taking calls on the phones, and Mel was at the computer. They were all dressed in their usual uniforms of jeans and bright-red sweatshirts, emblazoned with the words "TLC SQUAD – Give a Dog a Home"!

"Three months ago, the staff at the *Give a Dog a Home* kennel received an urgent call," the voiceover by Fiona Ramsay explained. "A local woman had found a young terrier lying

at the roadside, obviously injured and distressed. The TLC squad got on the case immediately."

The film switched to a shot of the TLC Squad jumping into their distinctive red van, and driving to the terrier's aid. Mandy and James exchanged looks of horror as the van stopped, and the camera zoomed in on the little dog lying in the gutter.

"Oh no!" Mandy gasped. The dog's reddish-brown, wiry coat was matted and bloodstained, and one of his back legs was hanging in a very awkward position. He was also very, very thin. His eyes were closed, and he was whimpering faintly.

"It looks like this poor little fellow has been hit by a car," Mel announced solemnly, after she'd done a quick examination of the terrier. "His leg might be broken, but our vet will have to check that out."

"It's possible that he's a stray," Lynn went on, as she gently stroked the dog's head with one finger, "because he's in very poor condition. But it's also possible that he was abandoned here, maybe even thrown out of a car by his original owner, and that's how he got injured."

"How can people be so cruel?" Mandy sat bolt upright, her face pale with anger and her fists clenched.

"I know," James agreed sadly. "But at least we know he must be OK, if he's going to be rehomed."

"That's true," Mrs Hope said gently.

The TLC squad had taken the terrier back to the kennel, where he was seen immediately by the *Give a Dog a Home* vet. The news was a mixture of good and bad. The dog's leg was broken, but it was a clean break, and the vet thought it would heal well. He was more worried by the fact that the little terrier was in very poor condition, and seemed half-starved.

"It's going to take a lot of tender, loving care to nurse this poor little pup back to health," Andy said, as the vet prepared to treat the dog's broken leg. "But that's what the TLC squad is here for!"

"And we've decided to call him Rusty, because of the colour of his coat," Mel added.

"Check back with us later in the programme to see how Rusty gets on!" Lynn finished off.

"Rusty! That's a lovely name," Mandy said, as the programme began showing the interview with Dr Richard Lacey, the dog psychologist.

"I bet lots of people are going to ring in and offer Rusty a good home!" James said eagerly.

Mandy and James always enjoyed the rest of *Give a Dog a Home*, with its mixture of interviews and interesting information about dogs, but tonight they were particularly impatient to find out what had happened to Rusty. They had to wait until about ten minutes before the end of the programme before he was mentioned again.

"And now, back to our featured dog." Fiona Ramsay smiled into the camera. "I'm sure you're all longing to know how Rusty's got on over the last three months—"

"We are!" Mandy said, bouncing impatiently up and down on the sofa.

"Well, let's take a look, shall we?" The presenter looked round, and called "Rusty!"

Two seconds later a little terrier was racing towards her, barking, his tail wagging madly from side to side. His coat was as shiny as if it had been polished, and he looked the picture of health. Beaming, Fiona Ramsay bent down so that Rusty could jump into her arms. He snuggled down happily, trying to lick the presenter's nose.

"Yes, this *is* Rusty!" Fiona Ramsay laughed. "I bet you can't believe your eyes!"

"I can't!" James pushed his glasses up his nose, and stared at the TV. "He ought to be called Shiny now, not Rusty! Doesn't he look great, Mandy?"

"Yes, he does." Mandy had a big lump in her throat. It was almost impossible to believe that it was the same dog. She couldn't help hoping that Rusty's former owners were watching. Then they would see what a difference a bit of loving care could make to a dog's life.

There was an interview with the vet, who confirmed that Rusty had made a full recovery, and then an interview with the TLC squad, accompanied by shots of Rusty being taken for a walk.

"Rusty's a great dog, full of life!" Mel said, smiling. "And he's very good with children."

"He can be noisy and boisterous," Andy pointed out. "But he's responding well to basic training."

Mandy and James laughed and applauded as Rusty obeyed the commands of sitting, staying and coming to heel, without putting a foot wrong.

"Rusty would make a wonderful pet," Lynn went on. "He needs a lot of attention, but he'll pay you back by giving you lots of love!"

There was a close-up of Rusty's appealing face as he looked up at Fiona Ramsay, before the presenter turned to the camera again.

"So, would you like to offer Rusty a loving new home? If you would, here's the number to ring . . ."

"I bet they'll get lots of calls!" James exclaimed, as the theme tune and end credits began.

"Of course they will!" Mandy agreed

immediately. She smiled as the programme finished with more film of Rusty playing happily with the TLC squad. "Who wouldn't want a cute little dog like Rusty?"

2

Holly and Mince Pies

"I wonder if Rusty's found a new owner yet," James said, as he and Mandy walked through the village to school the following morning.

"I think it probably takes quite a while," Mandy pointed out. "The *Give a Dog a Home* kennel will want to check people out carefully, to make sure Rusty gets just the right home."

"Yes, I suppose so." James shivered, and tucked his long stripy scarf more firmly into his coat. "It's cold, isn't it? Do you think it might snow?"

"I hope so!" Mandy said eagerly. A white Christmas would be perfect. They would be able to go sledging on Beacon Hill, and they might even be able to skate if the pool at the bottom of the hill froze solid.

"I hope Rusty gets his new home in time for Christmas!" James said, looking pleased. "Wouldn't that be great?"

"Hello, Mandy! Hello, James!"

Mandy and James turned round to see Libby Masters and her friend Ben Hardwick, both muffled up in woolly hats and scarfs, their noses red from the cold. They were a few years younger than Mandy and James, but they all knew each other well.

"Hi, Libby, hi Ben!" Mandy grinned. "How's Ryan, Libby?"

Libby's face lit up. She loved talking about her baby brother. "He's great!" she said enthusiastically.

Mandy smiled. She could remember a time when Libby hadn't been too happy at the thought of having a baby brother or sister, so it was nice to see how much she loved Ryan now.

"Did you see *Give a Dog a Home* last night?" Ben asked eagerly.

James nodded. "Yes, I watched it with Mandy. Wasn't Rusty brilliant?"

"Oh, he was great!" Ben said breathlessly. "I recorded the programme, and I watched it again this morning."

"Twice!" Libby said teasingly. "He was still watching it when I went round to call for him!"

"I'd love a dog like Rusty," Ben said wistfully.

Mandy glanced at James. They both knew that Ben was desperate for a dog, and had been for quite some time now. Mandy felt really sorry for him. She couldn't have a pet herself because her parents were so busy with the surgery, but at least she was always surrounded by animals at Animal Ark, even if they belonged to other people. But Ben didn't even have that.

"I wanted to ring up about giving Rusty a home," Ben went on sadly, as they all went into the school playground. "But Mum said no. She said terriers are too noisy."

"Well, most dogs can be noisy!" Mandy said carefully. "But you can always train them to be quiet!"

Ben nodded, still looking rather downcast. Libby took his arm. "Come on, let's go and join in with the rounders game."

"Poor Ben!" Mandy said, as the two younger

children ran off to join their classmates, who were playing rounders on the other side of the playground. "He wants a dog so badly."

"Do you remember what happened when the last series of *Give a Dog a Home* was on?" James asked. "Ben wanted to ring up about every single dog that was looking for a new owner!"

Mandy frowned. "Yes, and his mum always said no."

"That's right." James pushed his glasses higher up his nose. "She kept saying the dogs were too big, too small, too old, too noisy . . ."

"It sounds to me like Mrs Hardwick just doesn't like dogs much, and so she's making excuses," Mandy said thoughtfully.

Mandy and James looked at each other, and sighed. It certainly didn't look as if Ben was going to be Rusty's new owner. In fact, Ben's chances of getting a dog at all seemed very slim indeed.

"Only one more day to go!" James said with satisfaction, as he and Mandy joined the rush to escape from school at the end of the day. "I can't wait for the holidays!"

"Neither can I!" Mandy said enthusiastically. The day had been spent helping their teachers to clear up their classrooms, and put everything in order before the end of term. Mandy was relieved that they hadn't had to do any work, because she had been thinking about Ben all day, and wouldn't have been able to concentrate.

"I was wondering if there was anything we could do to help Ben," James said, as they left the school playground. "He's been on my mind all day."

Mandy nodded. "Me too!" Then she looked solemn. "Maybe I could ask Mum or Dad to talk to Mrs Hardwick about the kind of dog that would suit them. But Ben's mum might not like it."

James nodded. "Maybe she'll change her mind about Rusty anyway. After all, it *is* Christmas!"

"Oh, that reminds me," Mandy said suddenly, "I've got to call in on Gran and

Grandad. Gran's baked me some cakes for our class party tomorrow."

"I wish I was in *your* class!" James said enviously. He was a year younger than Mandy, and in the class below her. "I *love* your gran's cooking!"

Mandy grinned. "Don't worry, I'll save you some!" she promised as they made their way to Lilac Cottage.

Gran and Grandad were very busy with their preparations for Christmas. Grandad was arranging sprigs of holly on the mantelpiece, and Gran was hard at work in the kitchen. Lilac Cottage was full of the delicious smell of baking. And with the roaring fire, and twinkling fairy lights draped on the beautifully decorated tree in the corner, Mandy thought it all felt very Christmassy.

"Do you want some holly to decorate Animal Ark, Mandy?" Grandad asked, as he finished tucking the last sprig in place. "We've got plenty left. I managed to cut quite a bit this year before the birds ate all the berries!"

"That would be great, Grandad," Mandy said

with a grin. "But it's a shame for the poor old birds!"

"Don't worry," Grandad replied with a wink. "We've been putting out nuts for them for the last couple of weeks. I'll pop over tomorrow with the holly."

"I've made you some mince pies, a jam sponge and some little fairy cakes." Mandy's Gran bustled in from the kitchen, carrying some airtight tins. "Will that be enough?"

"Oh, brilliant, Gran. Thank you!" Mandy said gratefully.

"And here's a few mince pies for your class, James." Gran handed him a tin, too, and James's face lit up.

"Thanks very much, Mrs Hope!" he said.

"Now how about some mince pies and a cup of hot chocolate before you go?" Gran went on, and Mandy and James looked at each other in delight.

While they were eating, Mandy told her grandparents about Ben, and how much he wanted a dog.

"We saw *Give a Dog a Home* last night," Grandad said, sipping his chocolate. "That Rusty was a real character."

"Yes, he'd make a lovely pet," Gran agreed.

"I don't think Mrs Hardwick thinks so," Mandy sighed.

"You've got that look in your eyes again, Mandy!" Grandad teased her.

"What look?" Mandy wanted to know.

"The look that means you're going to try

271

and do something to help Ben!" Grandad smiled at her.

"If Mrs Hardwick doesn't like dogs, dear, there's not much you can do about it," Gran said, as she handed round the mince pies.

"Maybe Gran's right," Mandy said, as she and James left Lilac Cottage, feeling very warm inside, and full of mince pies. "Maybe Mrs Hardwick's *never* going to let Ben have a dog."

"You're giving up before you've even started!" James exclaimed. "That's not like you, Mandy!"

Mandy couldn't help smiling as they walked through the village. But, before she could say anything, something else caught her attention.

"Look, James!" she said, grabbing his arm. "Isn't that Ben?"

"Yes, it is!" James squinted through his glasses. "What is he doing?"

Ben was acting very strangely. He was wandering up and down the narrow street, stopping now and then to peer into every garden and alleyway. He was concentrating so hard on what he was doing that he didn't even notice Mandy and James.

"I don't know." Mandy frowned. "But I think we ought to find out. Come on!"

3

Poor Ben!

"Ben!" Mandy called, but she had to say his name twice before he heard her. "Ben, what on earth are you doing?"

Ben blushed a fiery red as he suddenly saw Mandy and James walking towards him.

"Nothing."

"Have you lost something?" James asked.

"If you have, we'll help you look," Mandy offered.

There was silence for a moment or two, as Ben shuffled his feet in embarrassment. "I was looking for a dog," he muttered at last.

"A dog!" Mandy exclaimed, surprised.

"Whose dog?" James asked.

"A stray dog." Ben bit his lip. "I just thought that if I could find a stray dog running about Mum would let me keep it."

Mandy glanced at James. Poor Ben must have been really desperate for a dog to spend ages out in the cold on the off-chance that he might find a stray pet. And, even if he did, would his mum have let him keep it?

"I don't think it's a good idea, Ben," Mandy said gently. "Even if you did find a dog, it might not be a stray at all, and then you'd have to give it back to its real owner."

Ben's face fell. "I hadn't thought of that."

"Haven't you been home yet?" Mandy asked, noting that Ben still had his schoolbag with him.

"No." Ben shook his head, as James glanced at his watch.

"It's getting pretty late," James pointed out. "Won't your mum be worried?"

Ben heaved a huge sigh. "Yes, I suppose I'd better get back."

"We'll walk you home," Mandy said, with a quick look at James to make sure he agreed. It was quite dark by now and, although Welford was a safe place to live, Mandy didn't think Ben's mum would like the idea of him wandering around looking for stray dogs. Anyway, it was an opportunity to talk to Mrs Hardwick.

"Ben!" As soon as they opened the gate to the Hardwicks' house, Ben's mum flung open the front door. "Where have you been? I was getting worried!"

Mandy didn't say anything, knowing it was up to Ben to tell his mum what he'd been doing.

"Sorry," Ben muttered sheepishly.

"Too busy playing football after school, I expect!" Mrs Hardwick said with a relieved smile. "Hello, Mandy. Hello, James. Thank you for walking Ben home. Would you like to come in for a drink and some biscuits?"

"Oh, yes please," Mandy said immediately. She wasn't hungry at all, but this was too good a chance to miss.

"I'll burst if I eat any more!" James whispered in her ear, as they followed Ben into the Hardwicks' living-room.

"I know, but it's all in a good cause!" Mandy whispered back.

Ben had hurried over to the TV, and was switching it on.

"Let's watch the *Give a Dog a Home* video," he said eagerly. "Just the bits about Rusty."

"Oh, Ben, not that programme again," Mrs Hardwick complained as she carried a tray of drinks and a plate of biscuits into the room. Ben was fast-forwarding to the part where Rusty was discovered injured by the roadside. "You've already watched it twice today!"

"But it's great, Mum!"

Mandy saw how intently Ben watched the programme, and how he couldn't take his eyes

off Rusty. She could also see the frown on Mrs Hardwick's face. Things didn't look good for Ben and his dream of owning a dog.

"This is my *favourite* bit!" Ben said happily, as the healthy, shiny-coated Rusty raced up and down with the TLC squad. They all watched right until the end when the telephone number for people who wanted to be the dog's new owner was given out, and then Ben turned to his mum. Mandy could guess what was coming next.

"Mum, can I ring the programme about Rusty? *Please!* There's still time!"

"Oh, Ben!" Mrs Hardwick looked very uncomfortable indeed. "We've already had this conversation. Dogs are more trouble than they're worth. And terriers are very noisy. Everyone knows that they're very yappy little dogs."

"But Rusty wouldn't be!" Ben said desperately. "I'd train him to be quiet."

"No, Ben!" said Mrs Hardwick, and there was such a sharp tone to her voice that Mandy was a bit surprised. "If you have a dog at all, it has to be the right one for *us*. We couldn't possibly have a noisy dog, so don't ask me about Rusty again, please."

Ben's face fell, but Mandy's ears had pricked up. It sounded like Mrs Hardwick might be willing to let Ben have a dog, if they could just find one that she didn't object to.

"Your mum's right, you know, Ben," Mandy said gently. "You have to make sure you choose the right dog for *you*."

"Exactly!" Mrs Hardwick agreed, sounding relieved. "After all, Ben, it would be awful if the dog didn't fit into our family and we had to get rid of it."

Mrs Hardwick's voice sounded a bit shaky as she said that. Mandy wondered why, but she didn't feel she could ask.

"So even if I can't have Rusty, can I choose *another* dog?" Ben asked eagerly.

"We'll see," Mrs Hardwick said vaguely. "We'll talk about it after Christmas."

Ben looked really disappointed, but he didn't say anything. Mandy and James said their goodbyes and went, leaving both Ben and Mrs

Hardwick looking rather glum.

"That sounded a bit more hopeful, didn't it?" James said, as they went through the gate.

Mandy sighed. "Well, Mrs Hardwick didn't exactly say that Ben could have a dog."

"No, I know," James agreed. "But if we can just find the right dog for Ben, then maybe she'll say yes!"

"Yes, maybe," Mandy replied. But she had a suspicion that Ben's mum was going to prove very hard to please . . .

When Mandy got back to Animal Ark, she popped into the surgery at the back of the house. The evening appointments had just started, and the waiting-room was already filling up with patients. Mandy said hello to Jean the receptionist, then she spotted Richard Tanner, who was in her class at school, patiently waiting his turn. He had his Persian cat, Duchess, in a basket on his lap. Duchess was crouched down in the basket looking miserable.

"Hi, Richard." Mandy bent down to take a

closer look at the cat. "What's wrong?"

"Duchess didn't eat anything today," Richard said glumly. "Then, when I got home from school, she looked so miserable, I thought I'd better bring her to Animal Ark."

"I hope she'll be OK for Christmas," Mandy said, poking her finger into the basket to try and stroke the white cat. But Duchess just stared listlessly at her.

"Richard?" Emily Hope opened the door to the consulting-room, looking very professional in her white coat. "I'll see Duchess now." She smiled as she spotted Mandy. "I think we're going to be flat out tonight, love! Every single appointment is booked!"

"Don't worry about me!" Mandy said cheerfully. She was used to Animal Ark taking up large amounts of her parents' time, and she didn't mind a bit. All that mattered was that sick animals got the help they needed to make a full recovery.

"Make yourself a sandwich if you get hungry," her mum told her, as she ushered an anxious Richard into the consulting-room.

"Oh, and your father picked up a Christmas tree today from Mr Fenton. So you can start decorating it if you like."

"Brilliant!" Mandy exclaimed. George Fenton owned a sawmill on the edge of the village, and at Christmas he sold trees at his workshop. The Hopes had bought their tree from him for as long as Mandy could remember – it had become a Christmas tradition.

Mandy wasn't hungry just yet, so she hurried into the living-room to take a look at the tree. As usual, it was the biggest one they could fit into the room, with just enough space for a silver star on top. Mandy grinned, and plunged her hands into the big box of decorations she and her mum had brought down from the loft the night before. Pulling out tinsel, glittering glass ornaments and silver baubles, she carefully began to decorate the tree, but her mind was only half on the job. She was still thinking about Ben and wondering if there was any way they could persuade Mrs Hardwick to agree once and for all that he could have a dog.

Then Mandy's face lit up. "Of course!" she

said to herself with a smile, as an idea began
to form in her mind.

4

Taking Care of Blackie

"There's Ben!" Mandy nudged James, as they walked into the school playground. She couldn't wait to put her plan into action. She had told James about it on the way to school, and he thought it was a brilliant idea.

"He's looking pretty miserable," James

287

observed as they went over to him.

"Well, it's too late for him to ring up about Rusty now," Mandy sighed, waving to Richard Tanner, who looked much happier this morning. Mandy's mum had told her that Duchess had a viral infection, and that the cat would be fine after a course of pills. "But I'm sure there's another dog somewhere who'd be just perfect for Ben!"

"Don't forget Mrs Hardwick," James reminded her, and Mandy nodded. It was just as important to please Mrs Hardwick as it was to find the right dog for Ben. But it certainly wasn't going to be easy.

"Hi, Ben," Mandy said warmly, as they stopped in front of the younger boy.

"Hello," Ben muttered, and Mandy's heart went out to him. He certainly was miserable.

"Are you looking forward to your class party?" James asked.

"I suppose so," Ben sighed, but he didn't seem too enthusiastic. Mandy hoped that what she had planned would make him feel a whole lot better.

"What are you doing tomorrow, Ben?" she asked.

Ben blinked at the unexpected question. "I don't know," he said. "Why?"

"Well, James and I are planning to go for a walk along the local nature trail in the morning," Mandy explained. "You know, the one that starts near Beacon Hill? We were wondering if you wanted to come with us."

Ben looked a bit more cheerful. "OK, I'll have to ask my mum, though."

"Maybe your mum would like to come along too," Mandy suggested. It was, in fact, very important that Mrs Hardwick came with them if Mandy's plan was going to work. "We have to have a grown-up with us, you see."

"All right." Ben nodded. "Shall I ask Libby to come too?"

"Yes, why not?" Mandy agreed.

"I'll go and ask her now." Ben was looking a lot happier. "And if Mum can't come, maybe Libby's mum will."

Mandy glanced at James. That wouldn't

work at all! They'd just have to hope that Mrs Hardwick agreed.

"Are you bringing Blackie, James?" Ben asked eagerly.

"Of course I am!" James replied.

Ben's eyes lit up. "Oh, great!" he exclaimed, as he raced off to find Libby.

Mandy and James looked at each other and laughed.

"Let's hope it all goes to plan tomorrow!" Mandy said. If all did go well, there was a chance that Ben would have his dog in time for Christmas.

"You want *me* to take care of Blackie on the walk?"

Ben's face was a picture of excitement, as he stared at James and Mandy with wide eyes.

"Well, you want to learn how to look after a dog, don't you?" James laughed, holding out Blackie's lead. "Go on, take it!"

Mandy watched, smiling, as Ben took hold of Blackie's lead as carefully as if it was made of glass. The puppy was already snuffling around in the hedgerow at the start of the nature trail.

It was a bright, frosty morning, and the grass was crisp underfoot. All the trees were white with frost, and even the spiders' webs hanging in the bushes were coated in glistening silver. Mandy thought it all looked beautiful. She took a deep breath of the clean, cold air, and glanced at Mrs Hardwick. Luckily Ben's mum had agreed to come with them.

"Good dog, Blackie," Ben said happily, patting the puppy's head, and Blackie stopped exploring long enough to give the young boy's hand a friendly lick.

Mandy watched Mrs Hardwick staring at Ben and Blackie with a very strange look on her face, and wondered what she was thinking.

"We need to go that way," Libby Masters said. She was studying the signs ahead of them. The trail was marked out with pictures of a squirrel nibbling a nut, so there was no chance of them losing their way.

"How long is the trail?" James asked, as they set off.

"About two kilometres," Mandy replied.

James groaned. "I hope I can keep up!" he said. "I'm still full from our class party yesterday!"

"Well, you shouldn't have eaten so many of Gran's mince pies!" Mandy teased him.

"It's lucky that I'm looking after Blackie today, then," Ben called as the puppy trotted along in front of everyone else, pulling Ben with him. "You can have a rest, James."

"Thanks, Ben," James called back.

"Wait for me!" Libby shouted, running to catch her friend and Blackie up.

Mandy wasn't sure that they would see much wildlife on the trail. Animals such as squirrels would probably have begun hibernating now that the cold weather had arrived. But there were still birds foraging for food, and a robin was perched in the lower branches of a tree, watching them with its bright eyes.

Anyway, Ben and Blackie certainly seemed to be enjoying themselves. Mandy watched as Blackie stopped to investigate an interesting smell at the base of a tree trunk. Ben took the

opportunity to pet and stroke the puppy, and Blackie immediately lost interest in the scent and happily allowed Ben to fuss him. Ben turned to say something to Libby, which Mandy couldn't hear, but it was obvious from his shining eyes and happy smile that he was enjoying himself enormously. Mandy glanced at Mrs Hardwick. Even she was smiling as she watched her son having so much fun.

"Blackie's a Labrador puppy, isn't he?" Mrs Hardwick asked suddenly.

"Yes," James agreed, and Mandy felt a sudden surge of hope. Mrs Hardwick taking an interest in Blackie might be a very good sign.

Ben's mum frowned. "Labradors are big dogs when they're fully-grown, aren't they?" she remarked. "Doesn't your mother mind, James?"

Mandy's heart sank. Why did Mrs Hardwick only ever seem to see the *bad* things about dogs?

"No, she loves Blackie," James said quickly. "And we've got room to have a big dog, too." He glanced at Mandy and added, "A Labrador wouldn't suit *everybody*."

"But there are lots of different kinds of dogs." Mandy was quick to jump in at this point. "Just like there are lots of different kinds of people."

"Yes, but unfortunately Ben always seems to want the *wrong* kind of dog!" Mrs Hardwick said quietly, watching Ben laughing as Blackie eagerly pulled him along.

"What do you mean, the wrong kind of dog?" Mandy asked politely. Just as she had hoped, bringing Ben and Blackie together had brought up the subject of dogs – and now that the conversation had begun, Mandy was determined to find out exactly why Mrs Hardwick was so reluctant to let Ben have a pet.

"Well . . ." For a change, Mrs Hardwick looked rather unsure of herself. "Dogs are a lot of work, and Ben always seems to want dogs that are too big or too small, for a start. We haven't got a very large house, so a big dog is out of the question. And I'd be worried about a small dog getting under my feet all the time."

"Well, there are lots of medium-sized dogs," Mandy pointed out gently.

"And Ben's bound to want a puppy," Mrs Hardwick went on. "I just don't have time to look after a puppy."

"I think Ben just wants a dog." James backed Mandy up firmly. "I don't think he'd mind if it wasn't a puppy."

"There are plenty of adult dogs in the animal shelters," Mandy pointed out. "And the staff there can tell you if they're quiet or noisy or whatever you want to know." She took a deep breath. It was now or never. "If we could find a nice, quiet, fully grown dog for Ben, do you think he might be allowed to have it?"

"Blackie!" Ben was helpless with laughter and so was Libby. Blackie had nosed his way into a hole in the hedgerow, and had come out with his ears white with frost, which made him look as if he'd been iced like a wedding cake. The puppy gave his head a vigorous shake, and Ben bent down and hugged him.

"You're great, Blackie!" he said. "I wish I had a dog like you!"

Mandy looked at Ben's mum, still waiting for an answer. Mrs Hardwick was smiling, but she looked sad too.

"I suppose a quiet, gentle dog wouldn't be too much bother," Mrs Hardwick muttered, almost to herself. "As long as it wasn't a puppy . . ."

Mandy's eyes lit up, and she glanced at James. He was also looking thrilled.

"Do you mean Ben *can* have a dog, Mrs Hardwick?" Mandy asked breathlessly.

"Well . . ." Ben's mum still looked

undecided. But, as she glanced at Ben and Blackie again, her eyes softened. "All right. Ben can have a dog – but only if we can find the right one!"

5

Freddie

"Mum! Do you mean it? I really can have a dog?"

Ben's eyes were shining, and he was staring at his mother as if he could hardly believe what she'd just told him.

"Now, don't get too excited, dear," Mrs Hardwick said quickly.

They had just dropped Libby off at Blackheath Farm where the Masters lived, and were on their way back to Welford. Mandy had hardly been able to stop herself from telling Ben that his mum had finally agreed to his requests for a dog, but she'd managed to keep quiet and let Mrs Hardwick tell him herself. It had taken her quite a while to get round to it, though. Mandy hoped that didn't mean she was changing her mind again.

"That's fantastic!" Ben bounced up and down in his seat, a big grin on his face. "Thanks, Mum! You're the best mum in the whole world!"

Mandy could see that Mrs Hardwick was pleased, even though she tried to speak quite sternly.

"Now calm down, Ben. Dogs are a lot of work, and first you've got to promise to look after it. And, as I said before, any dog we adopt has to be the right one for us—"

Ben wasn't listening. "Can we go to the animal shelter now, Mum?" he demanded. "And can Mandy and James come too?"

Mrs Hardwick looked rather shocked. "What, right now?" she exclaimed. "But it's lunch-time. I'm sure Mandy and James have other plans for this afternoon."

"No, we haven't," Mandy and James said together. Mandy was secretly starting to get a bit worried that Mrs Hardwick might change her mind if she had more time to think about it. The sooner Ben found his dog, the better.

"I was thinking of waiting until after Christmas—" Mrs Hardwick began, but Ben interrupted her.

"But I don't want to wait!" he complained. "I want to go now! Then we'll have the dog in time for Christmas!"

"You might not be able to, Ben," Mandy said gently. "Lots of animal shelters won't rehome dogs and puppies close to Christmas-time. It's so that they're not given as presents." Ben's face fell, and Mandy went on quickly. "But you can choose a dog now, even if you can't take it home until *after* Christmas."

Ben immediately cheered up again. "That's what we'll do, then!" he said firmly. "So can we go this afternoon, Mum? Please?"

Mrs Hardwick sighed, and gave in. "All right. But we'd better go home and have some lunch first. And Mandy and James will have to ring their parents, and check that it's all right with them."

In the back of the car, Mandy and James gave each other a secret thumbs-up sign. It looked as if Ben was going to get his dog after all, even if Mrs Hardwick did seem to be regretting her decision.

"So many dogs," Ben said, his eyes wide as he stared at the row of pens filled with animals. "I wish I could take them *all* home!"

"Don't let your Mum hear you say that!" Mandy laughed.

After lunch at the Hardwicks' house, they'd all driven over to Welford Animal Sanctuary, which was just outside the village. It was run by Betty Hilder, whom Mandy and James knew well. They'd had been there many times before, but to Ben it was all new. He was so excited, he could hardly keep still as they drew up outside Betty Hilder's bungalow.

"Of course you can come and look at the dogs," Betty had said warmly as she let them in. "I've got quite a few in at the moment. Go and have a look around."

The pens where the dogs and cats were housed were in the garden behind Betty's bungalow, and Ben had hurried out there straight away, followed by Mandy and James. Meanwhile Mrs Hardwick had stopped to chat to Betty for a few minutes.

"Mandy's right," Mrs Hardwick said, as she joined the three friends. "Betty says she won't rehome animals just before Christmas, but if we find one we like, we can collect it in the New Year."

Mrs Hardwick was sounding rather gloomy again, and Mandy glanced at her nervously. Surely she wasn't going to change her mind? Not now that they were actually at the shelter, and Ben was so close to his dream of getting a dog!

Feeling rather worried, Mandy followed the others over to the row of pens. Betty had been in the middle of mucking out the stables, and she'd gone back to it, saying they could call her if they wanted extra information about any of the dogs. Mandy rather wished that Betty had stayed with them. She had a feeling that Mrs Hardwick was going to be difficult to please.

Ben was ahead of everyone else, and was already looking eagerly into the first cage.

"Oh, look at this one!" he called. "It's so sweet!"

The dog was a little terrier, not unlike Rusty, except that his coat was more sandy-coloured. As Mandy and the others gathered round, he immediately rushed over to lick Ben's fingers through the wire mesh, barking loudly.

"Oh no, Ben!" Mrs Hardwick said firmly. "He's far too noisy! I've told you, I don't want any yappy little dogs!"

"All right," Ben agreed, without looking too disappointed. "There are lots of other dogs here!"

The next cage also held a very friendly dog, a medium-sized mongrel with a shaggy black-

and-white coat. He was lying in his bed in the corner, but when he spotted Mandy and the others outside he climbed to his feet and padded over to say hello.

"He's nice and quiet," Mandy pointed out, reading the sign on the front of the cage. "And he's called Bobby. Hello, Bobby!"

"He's really friendly too," Ben remarked, scratching Bobby's head through the wire mesh.

Mrs Hardwick frowned. "He looks quite old to me. We don't want an elderly dog – it could cause all sorts of problems."

"I don't mind," Ben said wistfully.

"Your mum's probably right," Mandy said. Even if Mrs Hardwick *was* just making excuses, an elderly dog wouldn't really suit Ben. "You want a dog you can run about with."

The next dogs they saw were two lively black-and-white puppies. Ben fell in love with them instantly, and so did Mandy and James, but Mrs Hardwick wouldn't change her mind.

"No puppies, Ben!" she warned him. "That's what we agreed."

Ben nodded and sighed. Mandy felt really sorry for him. Mrs Hardwick wasn't exactly being very helpful about choosing a dog. Surely she wasn't trying to get out of it now, after she'd agreed that Ben could have a pet?

The dogs in the next row of cages weren't right either. One was a Jack Russell, which of course was too small for Mrs Hardwick; three were mongrels, whom Ben's mum said barked too much; and one was an Irish wolfhound. Mrs Hardwick almost fainted when she saw how big he was.

"It's all right, Mum," Ben grinned. "I don't think *that's* the right dog for us!"

But Mandy could see that Ben was beginning to look worried as they continued to walk up and down, looking into the cages. Mrs Hardwick was indeed proving very difficult to please, as Mandy had thought she might – or was she just making excuses on purpose because she really didn't want Ben to have a dog at all?

"I like this one." Ben stopped suddenly in front of one of the cages, and Mandy and James hurried over to have a look at the dog. Mrs Hardwick followed.

As far as Mandy could tell, this dog was perfect! She was a cross-breed, of medium size, with a short, rough white and brown coat and large brown eyes. Mandy guessed that she was probably about two years old, so she wasn't a puppy either. As Ben bent down to make friends with her, she whined and pawed at the wire mesh, but she didn't bark loudly, as so many of the other dogs had done.

"Her name's Cindy," Ben said, his eyes shining with delight. "Look, Mum, isn't she *lovely*?"

"And she seems very quiet and gentle," Mandy added quickly.

"Yes, she does," Mrs Hardwick agreed thoughtfully.

"Can we go in and see her, Mum?" Ben pleaded.

Mrs Hardwick hesitated, then nodded. "I'll go and ask Betty," she said and went off.

Ben turned to Mandy and James, his face full

of excitement. "Cindy's just perfect for me," he said happily. "I know she is!"

"She certainly looks it," Mandy agreed, stretching out a hand to tickle Cindy under the chin.

But when Mrs Hardwick came back, she didn't have Betty with her. Ben's face fell as he saw his mother coming back alone.

"Cindy must already have a new owner," he muttered sadly.

"No, Cindy hasn't found a new home yet," Mrs Hardwick explained as she joined them again. "But she's got a heart condition, so she needs an owner who can give her extra-special care."

Mandy saw Ben's bottom lip begin to tremble. "I can look after her—"

"No, Ben," his mum said firmly. "The medication and the vet's bills will be very expensive. We just couldn't afford it."

Mandy knew that Mrs Hardwick was right. It would take a very special owner to look after Cindy properly. But still, she couldn't help feeling that Mrs Hardwick was secretly relieved that she had a good excuse to turn Cindy down.

Ben was very depressed at having to leave Cindy behind, but he brightened up a little as they went on looking. He spotted two other dogs that he liked: one a mongrel with a very cheeky face, and the other a quiet but nervous-looking whippet. But, just as Mandy had suspected, Mrs Hardwick found reasons to refuse both dogs. The mongrel was too boisterous, and the other dog had been too nervous to come up to them at first, which Mrs Hardwick didn't like.

"Well, that's that then," Mrs Hardwick said as they reached the end of the last row, and Mandy was sure she could hear a note of relief in her voice. "Never mind, Ben. We'll come back again in the New Year."

"It doesn't matter," Ben muttered, his face all screwed up as if he was trying not to cry. "I'll *never* get a dog now!" And he ran off towards the car.

"Ben!" Mrs Hardwick called, but he didn't stop.

Feeling very upset herself, Mandy glanced at James. He looked as distressed as she was.

"Oh dear," Mrs Hardwick sighed. "I just wish Ben could understand . . ."

"Understand what, Mrs Hardwick?" Mandy asked quietly.

"That dogs can be more trouble than they're worth!" Mrs Hardwick burst out. "And I should know!" Then she looked worried, as if she'd said more than she'd meant to.

"What do you mean?" Mandy asked.

Mrs Hardwick hesitated. "Oh, nothing," she muttered. "It's just that I had a dog myself when I was a little girl . . ."

"You did?" Mandy was surprised.

"Yes, his name was Freddie." Mrs Hardwick's face lit up briefly. "My father gave him to me, and I loved him so much. He was a mongrel puppy when we got him, and he was very small. Tiny, in fact. But, my goodness, he grew into the most enormous dog. Nearly as big as that Irish wolfhound!"

"And what happened?" James asked.

Mrs Hardwick looked depressed again.

"Freddie was noisy and boisterous. He used to bark all the time, and he ate us out of house and home. In the end, my father insisted on giving him away." She sniffed, and Mandy saw that there were tears in her eyes. "I've never forgotten it. It was so upsetting . . ."

Mandy glanced at James. So that was why Mrs Hardwick was always going on about finding the right dog – because she'd had such a bad experience in her own childhood.

"I don't know what I'd do if Ben's dog turned out to be as bad as Freddie," Mrs Hardwick said quietly. "I wouldn't want him to be as upset as I was."

"But if you make sure you get just the right dog for you—" Mandy began.

"Well, we thought Freddie was the right dog, and look what happened!" Mrs Hardwick sighed. "If only Ben would understand that dogs are a lot of bother!" she went on. "They're just not worth it."

Oh, yes, they are, Mandy thought fiercely. It was obvious now that Mrs Hardwick didn't really *dislike* dogs. She'd loved Freddie, after all. She was just very frightened about letting another dog into her life again. And, now that Mandy knew that, she was even more determined than ever to help Ben *and* his mum find the right dog for them.

6

Success!

"Ben still seems quite miserable," James said in a low voice to Mandy, as he helped her to clear the supper things off the table, one evening the next week.

"Yes, he does," Mandy agreed, keeping a sharp ear out for Ben, who had gone upstairs to the Hopes' bathroom. "I thought he might cheer up a bit as it's getting so close to Christmas, but he hasn't."

It was now just two days before Christmas Eve. Mandy and James hadn't seen much of Ben over the last few days, as they had both been helping their families to prepare for the seasonal festivities. Mandy and her parents had been Christmas shopping over the weekend, and so had the Hunters. But, even though they'd been really busy, Mandy had kept on racking her brains for a way to help Ben and Mrs Hardwick. She still hadn't come up with anything, though. The only thing she could think of to cheer Ben up was to invite him and James over to supper to watch the next *Give a Dog a Home*. It was the last edition of the show before Christmas.

"Are you two still worrying about Ben?" Mandy's father asked sympathetically, as he began to wash up the supper dishes.

Mandy nodded. "I just know Mrs Hardwick would love having a dog again!" she said, feeling frustrated. She had told her parents about Freddie, and how nervous Ben's mum was about getting another dog. "If only she would just give it a try."

"Well, at least she's said that Ben can *have* a dog," Mandy's mum pointed out, as she finished clearing the table. "That's something."

"Yes, but I think Mrs Hardwick wants to keep putting him off, hoping he'll forget about it!" Mandy replied. "There's not much chance of that, though!"

"Ssh, Ben's coming!" James hissed as he heard footsteps on the stairs.

"Is it nearly time for *Give a Dog a Home*?" Ben asked, as he came back into the kitchen. "I don't want to miss it."

"We've still got about five minutes," Mandy reassured him.

"I wonder which dog will be on tonight," Ben said eagerly, as the three friends settled themselves on the sofa next to the Hopes' glittering Christmas tree. Mandy smiled to herself as her parents joined them. If Mrs Hardwick thought that Ben might forget all about owning a dog, she was in for a very long wait!

"Oh, great!" Ben sat up straighter as the programme started, looking more cheerful. He stared intently at the TV screen, concentrating hard, and Mandy and James grinned at each other. The Christmas tree could have fallen on top of Ben's head and he wouldn't have noticed!

"And now, on to tonight's dog who needs a good home," Fiona Ramsay went on, having given a brief rundown on what else would be on the show that evening. "A few months ago, the TLC squad received a call from an elderly man, who was very upset about his dog, a Cavalier King Charles spaniel called Buster . . ."

"I like spaniels," Ben declared.

"Cavalier King Charles spaniels are lovely dogs," Mandy's dad agreed. "They're pretty active and quite intelligent."

On-screen, the TLC squad were hurrying to a run-down-looking house in the middle of a large, industrial city. A few moments later, Andy led a chestnut-coloured dog with long, floppy ears and a thick, plumy tail out of the house, followed by Mel and Lynn.

"This is Buster," Andy said, as the camera moved to get the dog in close-up. Buster looked fairly healthy and well fed, but his coat was matted and rather dirty. "He's a year old, and we think he's basically in good health, but his owner is elderly and has arthritis, and hasn't been able to groom him regularly."

"Buster's owner isn't able to live alone anymore, and is moving in with his son." Mel took up the tale. "Unfortunately, Buster can't go too, so he's looking for a new home."

"But first he needs a bit of tender, loving care from the *Give a Dog a Home* TLC squad!" Lynn added.

The vet confirmed that there was nothing wrong with Buster that a good grooming wouldn't cure. Then, as the film switched back to Fiona Ramsay telling viewers that there would be an update later, Ben turned to Mandy and James.

"Buster would be perfect for me!" he said excitedly. "He's not too big or small, he's not too old and he's not too loud!"

"Buster does seem like a quiet, well-behaved

dog," Mandy agreed cautiously. She didn't
want to raise Ben's hopes too much.

"What about your mum?" James wanted to
know.

"I'll ring her and ask right away!" Ben
jumped to his feet and raced out into the hall,
where the Hopes' phone was. A few seconds
later, he put his head round the door, looking
sheepish.

"Is it OK if I use your phone, Mrs Hope?"

"Of course!" Mandy's mum laughed. "But

don't you want to wait to see the update on Buster?"

Ben shook his head. "No, I just know Buster's the dog for me!" And he disappeared again.

"He seems pretty sure!" James said with a grin.

"Well, Buster *does* seem perfect!" Mandy said slowly. "As long as Ben realises that a lot of other people are going to want him, too."

Ben was on the phone to his mother for quite a while. Mandy and James couldn't hear what he was saying as they watched the rest of *Give a Dog a Home*, but Mandy couldn't help feeling worried. What excuse would Mrs Hardwick come up with this time?

But when Ben came back into the room, he was beaming all over his face.

"Mum said yes!" he announced triumphantly.

"That's great, Ben!" Mandy exclaimed.

"Come on, let's ring right now," Ben said impatiently. "I can remember the number."

"There's no point," Mandy told him. "The

lines don't open until the end of the programme."

Ben was obviously on tenterhooks, but he sat down to watch the rest of *Give a Dog a Home*. As usual, there was an update on the featured dog at the end of the programme. After a month or two with the TLC squad, Buster's coat was now gleaming and he was glowing with health. He certainly was a beautiful dog, Mandy thought, and he seemed lively without being boisterous. Just what Ben, and Mrs Hardwick, needed!

The phone number for new owners flashed up on the bottom of the screen as usual, and Ben leaped to his feet.

"Come on, we can phone now!" he said breathlessly, and rushed out of the room into the hall. By the time Mandy and James caught up with him, Ben was already dialling the number.

"It's engaged," he said in a disappointed voice, dropping the receiver with a clatter.

"Well, lots of other people are calling too," Mandy consoled him. "Try again."

But the line was still engaged. Mandy, James and Ben took it in turns to ring, but they spent the next twenty minutes trying to get through without any success. Mandy couldn't help wondering if Mrs Hardwick had just said that Ben could ring about Buster because she had guessed that his chances of getting through weren't too good.

"I think you'd better go and use the payphone in the surgery," Mrs Hope said gently, as she came out of the living-room fifteen minutes later. "Someone may have an emergency with a sick animal and not be able to get through to us."

"Sorry, Mum," Mandy said. When the surgery was closed, emergency calls came direct to the Hopes' telephone.

"Yes, sorry, Mrs Hope," Ben added.

Mrs Hope smiled as she gave Mandy a handful of coins. "Off you go – and good luck!"

It was strange being in the surgery with no one else around, but at least it meant they weren't stopping worried pet owners from being able to contact them, Mandy thought. She picked up the phone, fed in some coins and dialled the number. But it was engaged; the same as before.

"This is hopeless!" James said in despair, after they'd spent the next half-hour trying to get through. "Everyone in England must be ringing up about Buster!"

"Maybe we should give up," Ben suggested, as Mandy took the receiver from him and pressed the "redial" button yet again.

"No, not yet," Mandy said in a weary but determined voice. Then her eyes widened in shock. "It's ringing!"

Ben and James were too stunned to say anything. Quickly Mandy handed the phone over to Ben, as a pleasant-sounding operator came on the line and said, "Welcome to the *Give a Dog a Home* switchboard. Are you inquiring about registering as a possible owner for Buster, our featured dog tonight?"

"Yes, please!" Ben said breathlessly, giving Mandy and James a thumbs-up sign.

Mandy and James gathered round Ben, listening in as the operator asked him his name, age, address and phone number, and also checked that a parent had given him permission to make the call. Then she asked Ben to explain why he thought he would be a good owner for Buster.

"She says someone will ring me about Buster before Christmas!" Ben announced triumphantly, as he put the receiver down.

"Well, you still don't know what will happen yet," Mandy pointed out gently. She didn't want Ben to get his hopes up too much. "Lots of people have rung about Buster, and only *one* person can be his new owner."

"And that will be me!" Ben said confidently. "Buster and I are perfect for each other!"

Mandy sighed, and glanced at James. She hoped that Ben wasn't going to be disappointed yet again.

7

Mandy Has a Plan

"We'll be able to take Buster and Blackie for walks together!" Ben said happily as he held the Labrador puppy's lead tightly. "I hope they like each other!"

Neither Mandy or James replied. It was the following day, and they'd met up with Ben to take Blackie for a walk. All Ben had talked about was Buster, and how wonderful it was going to be when he finally got a dog of his own. Mandy had tried warning Ben over and over again that he might not be chosen as Buster's new owner, but Ben was sure he was going to be the lucky one.

"Just remember that, even if you don't get Buster, there are still plenty of dogs that need a good home," Mandy said carefully.

"Yes, and after Christmas the animal shelters are always looking for new owners," James

chimed in. "You'll have lots of dogs to choose from then."

Ben shook his head. "I won't need to go back to the shelter, because I'll have Buster! He's the perfect dog for me!"

Mandy sighed. Ben really had set his heart on the spaniel. She just hoped he was in with a chance.

"Mum said to come in and have a hot drink when we got back," Ben said as they reached the Hardwicks' house. Mandy and James accepted gratefully. It was the day before Christmas Eve, and the wind was bitingly cold.

"And maybe *Give a Dog a Home* will ring me this morning!" Ben looked anxious. "They said they'd call before Christmas, and that's only the day after tomorrow."

"A lot of people called about Buster," Mandy pointed out, "so it must take the kennel staff a while to go through all the details."

Mrs Hardwick was in the hall, taking off her coat, when they arrived at the front door.

"I just popped out to get a pint of milk," she explained. "It's cold, isn't it?"

"Did anyone from the programme ring, Mum?" Ben asked anxiously.

Mrs Hardwick shook her head. "Not while I've been here."

Ben glanced at the answering machine next to the telephone, and his eyes lit up. "There's a message!" he gasped, leaping forward to press the "play" button.

"Oh, it's probably your gran." Mrs Hardwick went to hang her coat up. "She said she'd ring today."

"Hello, this is the *Give a Dog a Home* switchboard—"

"It's them!" Ben yelled. "It's about Buster!"

"Ssh!" Mandy said, "We can't hear what they're saying!"

The message gave a phone number. They wanted Ben to ring them back as soon as he could. James wrote the number down, and Ben lifted the receiver with shaking fingers.

"I wonder if we'll be able to have Buster before Christmas," he said as he dialled the number. "I think I'll buy him a present just in case!"

Mandy sighed quietly. If Ben *wasn't* going to be Buster's new owner, it was best if he found out straight away.

"Hello?" Ben said breathlessly as the phone was answered at the other end. "Hello, it's about Buster . . . You left a message for me . . ."

There was silence for a moment, and then Ben's face fell. He seemed to be struggling not to cry and Mandy moved closer to him so that she could put a sympathetic hand on his arm. She glanced at Mrs Hardwick. Ben's mum looked relieved for a moment, but that quickly changed to concern because Ben was upset.

"—and so Buster will probably be rehomed with a young couple not far from his previous home." Mandy could hear what the operator was saying, now that she was standing close to Ben. "They have to be checked out more thoroughly before a final decision is made, but it looks as if Buster will have a very good home with them."

"Oh." There were tears in Ben's eyes now. "Well, thank you for letting me know—" He couldn't say any more. He quickly pushed the receiver into Mandy's hand, and his mum came over and put her arm round his shoulders.

"Thank you for taking such an interest in Buster, Ben," the operator went on, just as an idea popped into Mandy's head.

"This isn't Ben, it's his friend Mandy Hope," Mandy replied politely, wondering if Mrs Hardwick would possibly agree to her idea. "I was wondering – are the *Give a Dog a Home* kennels open to the public?"

"They certainly are," the operator told her. "The kennels are run like any normal animal shelter, except that we only have dogs here. But they're all looking for new homes."

Mandy's heart beat faster. "So do you have lots of dogs at the moment?"

"Yes, we do," the woman replied. "And we expect more in after Christmas, of course."

"Could you hold on for a moment, please?" Mandy turned to the others. "There are lots of dogs at the *Give a Dog a Home* kennels," she explained. "Maybe we could go and visit them. It would be fun to see where the programme

was filmed, even if Ben couldn't find a dog there."

"Oh, yes!" Ben said, cheering up immediately.

James grinned and nodded. "Brilliant idea, Mandy!" he said.

Mandy looked at Mrs Hardwick, who seemed in two minds.

"Aren't the kennels far away?" she asked with a frown.

"No, they're near York," Mandy replied. "I could ask my mum or dad to take us."

"Please, Mum!" Ben said eagerly. "Can we go tomorrow?"

"Tomorrow!" his mum repeated. "It's Christmas Eve tomorrow, and I've got lots to do."

Ben looked very disappointed. "But you *did* say I could have a dog, Mum!"

Mrs Hardwick looked very uncomfortable. "Well, all right then," she agreed reluctantly.

Mandy gave a sigh of relief, and spoke to the operator again. "Can I have the address of the kennels, please?"

As she wrote it down, Mandy secretly hoped that her plan would work. She wanted to cheer Ben up, but that wasn't the only reason why she had suggested a visit to the *Give a Dog a Home* kennels. Mrs Hardwick might start finding reasons to reject all the dogs she saw yet again, but this time she would have Andy, Mel and Lynn to deal with. And, if anyone could find the right dog to suit Mrs Hardwick, it was the TLC squad!

8

Full Steam Ahead!

"You want me to drive up to the *Give a Dog a Home* kennels tomorrow?" Adam Hope put down his newspaper and stared at Mandy and James.

"Well, only if you can, Dad," Mandy said hopefully. "Mrs Hardwick would probably take us, but she might find some excuse!"

"I suppose this is all about finding a dog for Ben?" Mandy's father said with a smile. "There are lots of other local animal shelters you can try, you know, without rushing off to York!"

"I know," Mandy agreed. "But I really want to see the kennels where the programme's made."

"I wouldn't mind seeing them myself, as it happens," Adam Hope said thoughtfully.

"And York isn't that far away, Dad," Mandy went on.

"True," Mr Hope agreed.

"And I just know that the TLC squad will be able to find a dog that Mrs Hardwick likes!" Mandy finished eagerly.

Her dad grinned. "Oh, you're going to bring in the big guns, are you? Well, let's see if the famous TLC squad will be able to help!"

"Does that mean you'll take us, then?" Mandy asked.

"All right, you're on," Mr Hope agreed. "But we'll have to leave early. The roads will be very busy with people going Christmas shopping and visiting relatives or whatever."

Mandy and James cheered.

"But only if your mum thinks she can cope with the surgery on her own tomorrow," Mr Hope added quickly.

"Of course I can," Mandy's mum agreed, coming into the room and overhearing the end of the conversation. "We don't have many appointments booked in at the moment."

"That's great!" Mandy said, giving her mum a hug and beaming at James. If all went to plan tomorrow, Ben would at least know he was getting a dog soon, even if it didn't arrive in time for Christmas . . .

"Morning, Mandy."

Gran was coming up the path of Animal Ark as Mandy opened the front door. It was the following day, and Mandy, James and Mr Hope were leaving bright and early for the journey to the *Give a Dog a Home* kennels in York. They were picking Ben and his mum up on the way.

"Hi, Gran." Mandy gave her a hug. "What are you doing here?"

"I'm going to do some last-minute Christmas shopping, and I wondered if your mum wanted anything," Gran told her.

"How's Grandad?" Mandy wanted to know.

"He's fine, except that he's convinced it's going to snow!" Gran replied. "He was out in the garden yesterday evening, covering up all the tender plants."

"It *does* look like snow," James said, squinting up at the grey-coloured sky.

"A white Christmas!" Mandy exclaimed. "That would be brilliant!" Ben and his quest

for a dog had taken up so much of her time since school had finished, Mandy had hardly had time to think about Christmas at all. But now she was beginning to feel excited. There was only one day to go! And if they could find Ben his dog today, Christmas would be utterly perfect.

"Come on, you two. We'd best be off." Adam Hope came out of Animal Ark, buttoning up his coat. "I want to try and beat the traffic if possible. Oh, hello, Mum."

"Where are you all off to?" Mandy's gran wanted to know.

"To the *Give a Dog a Home* kennels," Mandy replied. "We're going to find a dog for Ben."

"Yes, and one that Mrs Hardwick will like!" James added.

Gran smiled. "Get the TLC squad to sort it out, then," she advised, and Mandy grinned.

"That's exactly what we're going to do, Gran!" she said as she climbed into the Land-rover.

As they pulled up outside the Hardwicks'

house, Mandy could see Ben's face at the window, watching for them eagerly. A moment later, he came rushing out of the front door, followed by his mum.

"The weather forecast on the TV said it's going to snow today," Mrs Hardwick said anxiously, as she climbed into the passenger seat next to Adam Hope. "Maybe we shouldn't be going."

Ben's face fell, and Mandy couldn't help feeling rather annoyed. Mrs Hardwick was *always* making excuses where dogs were concerned!

"Well, it's not a long journey to York," Mandy's father reassured her, "and if the weather turns bad, we can easily head for home again."

Mandy crossed her fingers for luck inside her warm red gloves. *Please, don't let it snow until we've got back home*, she willed silently.

"I hope you find a dog today, Ben," James said in a low voice. Mandy's dad and Mrs Hardwick were discussing the weather, and weren't listening to them.

Ben sighed. "Even if I do, Mum will probably think of some reason why I can't have it."

Mandy smiled to herself. Ben didn't know that she intended to enlist the help of the TLC squad to deal with Mrs Hardwick's objections!

"Let's just wait and see, shall we?" she said.

In the front seat, Mrs Hardwick had begun telling Mandy's father about her childhood dog, Freddie. Mandy, James and Ben listened in silence as she explained how upset she'd been when Freddie had to be given away.

"That's a shame," Mr Hope commented, when Mrs Hardwick had finished the story.

"Yes, and that's why I keep telling Ben how important it is to get the *right* dog for us," Mrs Hardwick said firmly.

"True," Mr Hope agreed. "But it's also just as important that the *dog* gets the right home, too."

Mrs Hardwick was surprised. "What do you mean?"

"Well, although you loved Freddie, he wasn't the right dog for you," Mandy's dad went on.

"He was too big for your house, and too noisy. But you weren't the right owners for Freddie, either. He needed somewhere with more space, and it sounds like he got bored. That's why he barked so much."

"I never thought of that." Mrs Hardwick sounded shocked. "I know that my father gave him to some people who lived on a farm in the countryside, and they thought he was a wonderful dog. Of course, Freddie would have had lots of space to run about, and plenty to do on a farm."

"The dog has to be right for the owner, and the owner has to be right for the dog," Adam Hope said gently. "It has to work both ways."

Mrs Hardwick was silent for a long time after that. Mandy wondered what she was thinking. Maybe now she would see that it was no one's fault that Freddie hadn't fitted into her family, and hopefully she wouldn't be quite so worried about letting Ben choose a dog.

As they drove the last few kilometres towards York, Mandy, James and Ben were on the lookout for the first sign to the *Give a Dog a*

Home kennels. It was in the countryside, just outside the city.

"There it is! There it is!" Mandy and Ben called out together, as Mr Hope joined the long queue of traffic leading up to a large roundabout.

"And we're only three kilometres away," James added.

As the Land-rover finally turned into the kennels car park, Mandy felt her tummy turn over with excitement. There was the familiar entrance where Fiona Ramsay stood every week to introduce the beginning of the programme. The TLC squad's red van was parked in one of the spaces, but there weren't many other cars about.

"I think we picked a good day to visit," Mandy's dad remarked, as they all climbed out of the Land-rover. "Most people will be out finishing their Christmas shopping."

"I should be able to get a good look at all the dogs, then!" Ben said eagerly.

Mandy glanced at Mrs Hardwick. She still looked a little nervous, but not as worried as she had been when they went to the local animal sanctuary. Mandy began to feel a bit more hopeful.

They all went through the main entrance and into the kennels' reception area.

"It's a lot smaller than it looks on TV, isn't it?" James whispered to Mandy and Ben, as they all went over to the reception desk.

"I wonder if the TV crew are filming here today," Ben said eagerly.

Mandy was longing to see if any of the TLC squad were manning the desk, but she was disappointed. The receptionist, a small, plump woman with glasses and brown hair, was very nice, though, and explained that they could wander around and look at the dogs on their own. And if there was one they liked the look of, they would be able to go in with a kennel-hand and get a closer look.

"Are the TV people filming here today?" Ben asked.

The receptionist shook her head. "No, the current series was filmed a while ago. They'll be filming a new series sometime after Christmas."

As everyone else went over to the entrance to the kennels, Mandy lingered at the reception desk.

"Are the TLC squad here this morning, please?" she asked in a low voice.

"Yes, they're around somewhere," the receptionist replied, with a twinkle in her eye. "Even though they're TV stars now, they still have to help with cleaning out the kennels! But if you want their autographs, just ask!"

"Thank you," Mandy said, and ran to catch

the others up. It would be nice to get the TLC squad's autographs, but that wasn't the most important thing. Most of all she wanted them to convince Mrs Hardwick that somewhere in the kennels was the perfect dog for Ben, and for her!

9

A Bit of TLC

"Oh, Ben, I don't think that dog will do at all!" Mrs Hardwick held up her hands in horror. "He's far too noisy, and look how dirty he is! He obviously enjoys rolling in the mud!"

Mandy sighed. The dog they were looking at was a handsome black-and-white Border collie, but he was certainly not the pet for Mrs Hardwick.

So far they had walked round half of the large kennels, and they hadn't yet found a dog that Ben and his mum could agree on. Mrs Hardwick was obviously trying hard to be more open-minded, but she still seemed very nervous that they might make the wrong decision. She examined every dog that they saw carefully, before deciding that something or other was wrong with it. Mandy longed to say that dogs were just like humans – people weren't perfect, either! But she thought that might sound a bit rude, so she kept quiet.

There was no sign of any of the TLC squad, which was also worrying Mandy. How could she ask them to help, if they were nowhere to be seen?

"Look at this one!" Ben had stopped in front of the last kennel in the row, and was staring in. A fluffy white dog, which looked as if it might be part poodle, trotted over to the front of the cage to say hello.

"She's cute!" Ben said, pushing his fingers

through the wire mesh to scratch the dog's head. "What do you think, Mum?"

"Oh, Ben, not a white dog!" Mrs Hardwick exclaimed. "Think how dirty it would get!"

James looked at Mandy and shrugged his shoulders, while Mr Hope raised his eyebrows.

"This is hopeless!" James whispered to Mandy. "Mrs Hardwick is *never* going to give in!"

Mandy thought that James was probably right. Even the talk Mandy's father had had with Mrs Hardwick during the journey hadn't done the trick. As everyone else moved on to the next row of kennels, Mandy lingered behind to stroke the little white dog.

"Sorry," she murmured as the dog looked up at her with big, brown eyes, "but I don't think even a Crufts Supreme Champion would please Mrs Hardwick!"

As Mandy hurried on to catch up with the others, she suddenly heard a soft little bark. Puzzled, she stopped and looked around. It sounded very close, and she wasn't that near to any of the kennels. Then she noticed she was standing next to a small shed. There was one at the end of each row of kennels, but Mandy had no idea what they were for. Then she heard it again, the same soft little bark.

The window was quite high, but Mandy grabbed hold of the ledge, and hauled herself up. Unfortunately the glass was quite misted on the inside and she couldn't see very much. But as Mandy stared in she could just make out a shaggy chestnut-coloured body, and a tail wagging like crazy. There was a dog in there!

"Can I help you?" said a voice from behind her.

Mandy was so surprised, she let go of the window ledge and crashed to the ground. She was even more surprised when she looked round to see Andy, Mel and Lynn, holding buckets and brooms and smiling at her. It was the TLC squad.

"Are you all right?" Mel asked, hurrying forward to Mandy. "Sorry we startled you."

"I'm fine!" Mandy gasped. She stared at Andy, Mel and Lynn as if she couldn't quite believe that they were real. It was very strange to meet someone you'd only seen on TV, Mandy thought. But the TLC squad seemed just as friendly and down-to-earth as they did on the programme.

"Are you looking for a dog?" Lynn asked with interest.

"No – I mean yes!" Mandy tried to get her breath back. "Well, my friend, Ben, is, but his mum doesn't like any of them. I wondered if you could help."

"You'd better tell us the whole story," Andy said gently.

Quickly Mandy told the TLC squad exactly what had happened. "And I think Mrs Hardwick would really love to have a dog," Mandy ended up. "But she's just so scared that Ben will choose one that isn't right for them."

"I see." Andy grinned at Mandy, then nodded at Lynn and Mel. "Well, I think you might have already solved this problem on your own, Mandy, without our help!"

"What do you mean?" Mandy asked, puzzled.

But before Andy could say anything else, Ben, Mrs Hardwick, Mr Hope and James came hurrying back to look for Mandy.

"There you are," Ben exclaimed. "We thought you'd got lost." Then his jaw dropped. "It's the TLC squad!" he stammered.

"At your service!" said Andy, giving a sweeping bow.

"Wow!" gasped James, shoving his glasses up his nose so he could get a better look. "It really is you!"

"Which one of you is Ben?" Lynn asked.

"I am," Ben said immediately.

"We hear you're looking for a pet," Mel said. "Would you like to tell us exactly what kind of dog you're hoping to find?"

"Well . . ." Ben glanced sideways at his mum. "I just want a dog I can play with and take for walks, but Mum doesn't want a noisy dog, and she doesn't want one that's too big or too small. It can't be white either, because it will get too dirty. And she doesn't want a puppy, or an old dog. Oh, and it mustn't have anything wrong with it."

Mrs Hardwick turned red and gave an embarrassed smile. "Oh dear. You must think I'm very fussy!" she muttered.

"Not at all," Lynn reassured her. "It's much better to know exactly what sort of dog you *do* want."

"And why do you think a dog would like to come and live with you?" Mel asked Ben's mum. Mandy grinned as Mrs Hardwick's mouth fell open. She obviously hadn't expected that!

"Well – er—" Mrs Hardwick faltered. "We've got a nice house and quite a big garden. And I'm at home in the daytime, so the dog wouldn't be left on its own."

"That's good," said Andy approvingly. "So you're looking for a quiet, well-behaved dog, who's perhaps had some basic training?"

"Well, yes." Mrs Hardwick nodded, as Mandy and James glanced at each other and smiled. The TLC squad was really putting Mrs Hardwick on the spot!

"Problem solved!" Lynn beamed. "Mandy's already found the perfect dog for you!"

"I have?" Mandy gasped.

"You have?" Ben cried.

"Yes, come this way!" said Andy, leading everyone over to the little building Mandy had been looking into. "This is one of the temporary sheds where we house the new arrivals while we prepare their kennels."

Mandy's eyes opened wide as she remembered the chestnut-coloured dog she had caught a glimpse of inside the shed.

"Sasha only came in this morning," Andy went on, as he unlocked the door. "She's a Cavalier King Charles Spaniel."

"Just like Buster!" Ben's face lit up.

"She's only two years old, but she's had some basic training and she's very quiet and well-behaved for such a young dog." Andy pushed open the door, and smiled at Mandy, Ben and James. "Why don't you go in and say hello?"

Her heart beating fast, Mandy followed James and Ben into the shed. There, waiting for them and wagging her tail, was one of the most adorable dogs Mandy had ever seen. Her coat was silky and well groomed, and her eyes were bright and intelligent.

"Oh, she's perfect!" Mandy gasped.

"She's a lovely dog," James added. But Ben was speechless; all he could do was stand and stare.

"Come on, Ben!" Mandy encouraged him gently as Sasha, eager to be stroked, padded over to them on her shaggy paws. "Say hello to her."

Ben knelt down, and Sasha rubbed her head on his knee. She was obviously a very friendly dog, without being at all boisterous and unruly.

"She's just what I want!" Ben said in a choked voice.

The TLC squad, Mr Hope and Mrs Hardwick were watching from the doorway, as the shed wasn't really big enough for them all to cram inside. Mandy looked at Ben's mum to see her reaction. She was staring down at Ben and Sasha, who was sitting quietly, allowing them all to stroke her and enjoying every minute of it.

"I'm a vet, so do you mind if I have a quick

look at her?" Adam Hope asked the TLC squad.

"Not at all," Andy said. "Our own vet hasn't examined her yet, so we'd be interested to know what you think."

Mandy watched with her heart in her mouth as her father gave Sasha a quick examination. If there was anything wrong, her dad would say so, even if it meant Ben wouldn't be able to have the spaniel. Ben was looking very nervous indeed, and Mandy gave him a reassuring smile. From what she could see, Sasha looked in the best of health, but the final word was down to her father.

"She's certainly got a lovely personality," Adam Hope remarked, as he finally released the spaniel. "She put up with me examining her without a murmur – I wish all my patients were like that!"

"What do you think, Dad?" Mandy asked urgently.

"She's in excellent condition," Mr Hope said, and Mandy, Ben and James all sighed with relief. "She's obviously been well-looked after."

"She belonged to a young couple who've gone travelling the world for a couple of years," Mel explained. "They hated parting with her, but they just didn't have any relatives or friends who could look after her for that length of time."

"So what do you think?" Lynn asked, and the three members of the TLC squad turned to look intently at Mrs Hardwick.

Ben's mum turned pink. "Well—" she began, then stopped.

Everyone waited to hear what Mrs Hardwick had to say. Mandy's heart began to race and she crossed her fingers firmly behind her back. What would Ben's mum decide?

10

And a Happy New Year!

"Well—" said Mrs Hardwick again. At the moment she didn't seem able to say anything else.

As Mandy looked at Mrs Hardwick staring down at Sasha, she suddenly had a brain-wave.

"Go on, Sasha!" she whispered, giving the

dog a gentle push towards Ben's mum. "It's now or never!"

Obediently, Sasha trotted across the shed towards Mrs Hardwick. She stopped at her feet, and waited politely for Ben's mum to reach down and pet her.

"Goodness me, she *is* very well-behaved, isn't she?" Mrs Hardwick said in amazement. "I hate those dogs that jump up at your legs."

As if she was agreeing with her, Sasha gave a soft little bark and gently licked Mrs Hardwick's fingers.

"She likes you, Mum!" Ben pointed out happily.

Everyone waited in silence as Mrs Hardwick continued to fuss Sasha. Mandy could see that Ben's mum was smiling, and she kept her fingers crossed. If ever there was a dog who could melt Mrs Hardwick's heart, it had to be this beautiful little spaniel.

"I think Sasha's already decided who her new owners are going to be!" Mel said with a grin. "But it's up to you, of course!"

Ben stared at his mum with a pleading look

on his face. "Can Sasha be our dog, Mum? Please?"

Mrs Hardwick looked at her son, and then down into Sasha's trusting brown eyes. "I think we've found the perfect dog for us at last, Ben," she said with a shaky smile.

"Oh, thanks, Mum!" Ben gasped with delight, and hurled himself across the shed to give Mrs Hardwick a big hug. Meanwhile Sasha's tail wagged madly from side to side,

and Mandy and James glanced at each other in delight. Ben had got his dog at last, and she was a beauty!

"Congratulations." Andy shook hands with Ben and his mother. "You couldn't have chosen a better dog!"

"I won't be able to take her home for Christmas though, will I?" Ben asked, picking Sasha up and hugging her. The spaniel didn't mind at all, and lay quietly and contentedly in her new owner's arms.

Mandy felt so pleased, she could almost burst. It had been worth all the trouble they had gone to, just to see the thrilled look on Ben's face.

"I'm afraid not," Mel told him. "You'll have to wait till the New Year, and there'll also have to be a home check."

"But we don't live in York!" Ben said, suddenly looking rather worried.

"That's OK," Andy reassured him. "Because of the programme, our new owners come from all over the country. If we can't get to you, we usually ask your local animal shelter to do the home check and report back to us."

"I wish I didn't have to leave you here over Christmas, Sasha," Ben whispered in the spaniel's silky ear. "But I'll buy you lots of presents, and you can have them later."

"Just a minute, Ben." Lynn had slipped away from the shed a few minutes before. Now she had returned with a Polaroid camera in her hand. "If you like, we can take your picture with Sasha, so that you've got a reminder of her until she comes to live with you."

"Yes, please." Ben flushed with pleasure, as everyone moved out of the way so that Lynn could get a good shot of him and the spaniel. "But I want you to be in the photo as well, Mandy," Ben went on. "If it wasn't for you, I'd never have found my perfect dog!"

Mandy blushed, and went to stand next to Ben.

"Right, look this way!" Lynn called as she looked through the lens, and they did as she said – even Sasha. The picture slid out of the camera and, after it had developed, Lynn handed it to Ben.

"I'll pin this up in my bedroom as soon as I get home," Ben said proudly. "Doesn't Sasha look cute, Mandy?"

"She's gorgeous," Mandy agreed.

"Look!" James gasped, pointing at the window. "It's snowing!"

Mandy glanced outside. Sure enough, large white snowflakes were floating slowly down to the ground.

"It's snowing, and I've got a dog!" Ben said happily as he carefully put Sasha down. "This is going to be the best Christmas ever."

"Thank you very much," Mandy said to the TLC squad, and Ben nodded.

"Not at all." Andy shrugged. "*You* were the one who found Sasha, Mandy."

"Let us know how Sasha gets on, won't you?" Mel said.

"And keep watching *Give a Dog a Home!*" Lynn added.

Mrs Hardwick looked at Mandy and James. "Thank you for all your help," she said with a smile. "And you too, Mr Hope."

Mandy grinned at Ben as the spaniel padded

over to them for one last goodbye cuddle. She couldn't have asked for a better Christmas present than seeing Ben's joyful face as he stroked his new dog.

"Bye, Sasha," Ben said, fondling the spaniel's silky coat. "I'll see you again very soon."

"Bye, Sasha," Mandy whispered. "And Merry Christmas!"

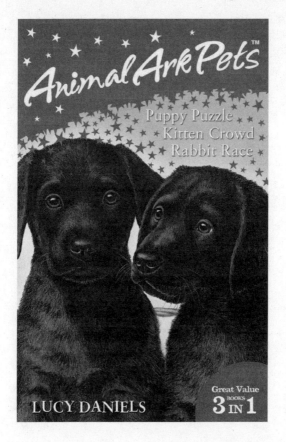

Three Animal Ark Pets books in one! In *Puppy Puzzle* two
identical Labrador puppies are in a muddle! One of them has
gone missing - but which one is it? Six newborn kittens are
without a home in *Kitten Crowd* – can Mandy find them new
owners by the end of the week? Whilst in *Rabbit Race* a baby
rabbit is in danger, and only Mandy and James can help ...

For the full range of Animal Ark Pets
and Animal Ark books please visit

www.hodderchildrens.co.uk

Animal Ark Pets™

Pony Parade
Guinea-pig Gang
Gerbil Genius

LUCY DANIELS

Great Value
3 BOOKS IN 1

Paul's new pony is from a sanctuary, when people at school see it, they think he's been mistreating his pet. Can Mandy prove them wrong in *Pony Parade*? In *Guinea-pig Gang* Mandy has lots of friends with guinea-pigs and together they form a gang. But Lisa won't join in with her pedigree guinea-pig. Why is she being so snooty? In the exciting adventure *Gerbil Genius* Mandy and James find an escaped gerbil out in the wild. Can they tame him and get him used to humans again?

For the full range of Animal Ark Pets
and Animal Ark books please visit

www.hodderchildrens.co.uk

Follow Mandy's adventures with another great value set from
Animal Ark Pets! Libby's pet hen has stopped eating, and
Libby's really worried about her. Can Mandy find a way to
cheer them up? Find out in *Chick Challenge*. In *Hamster Hotel*
Mandy promises to help her grandparents look after a friend's
hamster – but even she has a problem when the hamster
disappears! *Mouse Magic* sees Mandy come up with a plan to
make a pet mouse the star of the school play . . .

For the full range of Animal Ark Pets
and Animal Ark books please visit

www.hodderchildrens.co.uk